A Candlelight Ecstasy Romance®

"MORGANA, I HAVE A SURPRISE FOR YOU," NICHOLAS SAID EXCITEDLY. "I'VE DECIDED TO BECOME YOUR NEW BUSINESS PARTNER."

"That's your surprise," she said quietly.

"Well, yes." Caution edged his voice. "I really thought you'd be pleased."

"Get away from me!" Morgana fiercely pushed him away.

"Morgana, please wait. I have something more to say."

"I've heard enough, Nicholas Bedford! I can't believe you did this to me! I trusted you!"

"You're not looking at this logically," Nicholas insisted.

"Did you plan to buy my sister's half of the business behind my back or not, Nicholas?" Morgana demanded.

"Yes, technically, I guess I did, but I also wanted—"

"So you've bought my business! Well, it'll be a cold day in hell when you get to run it!"

CANDLELIGHT ECSTASY ROMANCE®

234 A BETTER FATE, *Prudence Martin*
235 BLUE RIDGE AUTUMN, *Natalie Stone*
236 BEGUILED BY A STRANGER, *Eleanor Woods*
237 LOVE, BID ME WELCOME, *JoAnna Brandon*
238 HEARTBEATS, *Jo Calloway*
239 OUT OF CONTROL, *Lori Copeland*
240 TAKING A CHANCE, *Anna Hudson*
241 HOURS TO CHERISH, *Heather Graham*
242 PRIVATE ACCOUNT, *Cathie Linz*
243 THE BEST THINGS IN LIFE, *Linda Vail*
244 SETTLING THE SCORE, *Norma Brader*
245 TOO GOOD TO BE TRUE, *Alison Tyler*
246 SECRETS FOR SHARING, *Carol Norris*
247 WORKING IT OUT, *Julia Howard*
248 STAR ATTRACTION, *Melanie Catley*
249 FOR BETTER OR WORSE, *Linda Randall Wisdom*
250 SUMMER WINE, *Alexis Hill Jordan*
251 NO LOVE LOST, *Eleanor Woods*
252 A MATTER OF JUDGMENT, *Emily Elliott*
253 GOLDEN VOWS, *Karen Whittenburg*
254 AN EXPERT'S ADVICE, *Joanne Bremer*
255 A RISK WORTH TAKING, *Jan Stuart*
256 GAME PLAN, *Sara Jennings*
257 WITH EACH PASSING HOUR, *Emma Bennett*
258 PROMISE OF SPRING, *Jean Hager*
259 TENDER AWAKENING, *Alison Tyler*
260 DESPERATE YEARNING, *Dallas Hamlin*
261 GIVE AND TAKE, *Sheila Paulos*
262 AN UNFORGETTABLE CARESS, *Donna Kimel Vitek*
263 TOMORROW WILL COME, *Megan Lane*
264 RUN TO RAPTURE, *Margot Prince*
265 LOVE'S SECRET GARDEN, *Nona Gamel*
266 WINNER TAKES ALL, *Cathie Linz*
267 A WINNING COMBINATION, *Lori Copeland*
268 A COMPROMISING PASSION, *Nell Kincaid*
269 TAKE MY HAND, *Anna Hudson*
270 HIGH STAKES, *Eleanor Woods*
271 SERENA'S MAGIC, *Heather Graham*
272 A DARING ALLIANCE, *Alison Tyler*
273 SCATTERED ROSES, *Jo Calloway*

THE PERFECT AFFAIR

Lynn Patrick

A CANDLELIGHT ECSTASY ROMANCE®

Published by
Dell Publishing Co., Inc.
1 Dag Hammarskjold Plaza
New York, New York 10017

Dell ® TM 681510, Dell Publishing Co., Inc.

Candlelight Ecstasy Romance®, 1,203,540, is a registered trademark
of Dell Publishing Co., Inc., New York, New York.

ISBN: 0-440-16904-6

Printed in the United States of America
First printing—October 1984

To everyone who said to keep trying

To Our Readers:

We have been delighted with your enthusiastic response to Candlelight Ecstasy Romances®, and we thank you for the interest you have shown in this exciting series.

In the upcoming months we will continue to present the distinctive, sensuous love stories you have come to expect only from Ecstasy. We look forward to bringing you many more books from your favorite authors and also the very finest work from new authors of contemporary romantic fiction.

As always, we are striving to present the unique, absorbing love stories that you enjoy most—books that are more than ordinary romance.

Your suggestions and comments are always welcome. Please write to us at the address below.

Sincerely,

The Editors
Candlelight Romances
1 Dag Hammarskjold Plaza
New York, New York 10017

To Our Readers:

We have been delighted with your enthusiastic response to Candlelight Ecstasy Romances™, and we thank you for the interest you have shown in this exciting series.

In the upcoming months we will continue to present the distinctive sensuous love stories you have come to expect only from Ecstasy. We look forward to bringing you many more books from your favorite authors and also the very finest work from new authors of contemporary romantic fiction.

As always, we are striving to present the unique, absorbing love stories that you enjoy most—books that are more than ordinary romance.

Your suggestions and comments are always welcome. Please write to us at the address below.

Sincerely,

The Editors
Candlelight Romances
1 Dag Hammarskjold Plaza
New York, New York 10017

CHAPTER ONE

Adding the final box of flowers to the pile, Morgana Lawrence blew a sigh of relief as though it might cool her flushed face. She checked the thermostat: eighty-six degrees. That worried her. If the temperature didn't drop rapidly, she would be stuck with hundreds of wilted orchids and gardenias in the morning.

Pulling her sweat-soaked hair away from her face, Morgana pinned up her black tresses. She usually refused to wear her hair that way since it accented her long neck, but she was too hot to care. Longing to do nothing more than strip off her skimpy T-shirt and shorts and jump into a refreshing shower, Morgana picked up her clipboard instead. It wouldn't hurt to do one more inventory.

Everything had to be perfect for the sunrise wedding ceremony. Although she tried to ignore the chattering chimp and screeching birds, it was impossible. With a sigh of resignation Morgana crossed the room, opened the cage door, and held out her hand.

"Come on out, you little creep," she said to the chimp.

Like a small child that knows it has won its way, the chimp eagerly took her hand and waddled alongside her.

"I don't think they'll miss one banana, do you?" She lifted a bunch from one of the dozens of crates stacked along the walls. He took the fruit she offered him, then, engrossed in removing the peel, sat quietly.

"If only you two could be silenced so easily." She scolded the macaw and cockatoo. Their screeching was giving her a royal headache!

"I'll be glad when this wedding is over," Morgana complained as she eyed the clutter. Would the van hold all this? Across the room the phone rang. Morgana glanced at the chimp before going to find it. He was absorbed in eating his banana. She was sure he'd be all right for a moment.

Unable to see the telephone, Morgana followed the cord to its hiding place behind the boxes of flowers she had stacked so carefully. She hunted for the phone anxiously, hoping the caller would hang on for a few rings longer. In her haste she managed to dump an entire box of orchids around her feet.

"Damn!" Her hand closed over the receiver. "Hello. Lawrence and Smythe, Fantasy Weddings."

"Wake here."

"Oh, Mr. Wake." Morgana was relieved to hear from him. She had tried unsuccessfully to reach him all day. "The deliveries have been made, and everything's ready for tomorrow," she said, assuring him with her fingers crossed.

"Miss Lawrence, I don't know quite how to tell you this, but I have some news for you."

"Another change?" she asked wearily, pulling her hand across her forehead. She couldn't believe her luck. Every time she thought everything was set, the Wakes threw her another curve. If it weren't for the money . . .

"Mr. Wake, I'll do the very best I can, but it *is* Saturday afternoon. That only leaves us about thirteen hours—"

He interrupted her. "The jungle wedding is off."

"What?"

12

"Lavinia and I have decided to elope."

"Elope?" The word came out in a strangled sob. She'd gone through all this for nothing?

"The family's impossible, just like the first time we got married. We eloped then, too."

"Mr. Wake, the wedding is scheduled for sunrise. Everything had to be delivered *here.* At my shop!" Morgana waved her free hand in agitation. "I'm surrounded by crates of fresh fruit, gallons of piña colada mix, boxes of flowers, one screeching chimp, and two squawking birds!" On cue each animal tried to outdo the other, so Morgana used her free hand to cover her left ear. "What do I do with all this?"

"Sell everything," Mr. Wake said.

"What?"

"We're leaving for Africa tonight," Wake told her. "We'll be married at the safari camp where we reconciled. My bush outfit and Lavinia's suede wrap dress will be a little fancy for the real jungle, but we'll wear them anyway. You did do a nice job designing them," he conceded, as if playing up to her ego would smooth over things.

Morgana found herself in the middle of a nightmare. There had never been a cancellation before. She'd sensed this wedding would be trouble, but she'd gone along with her sister when Blanche enthusiastically accepted the Wake wedding, assuring the reconciled couple their ideas were perfectly within reason.

"Mr. Wake, there are outstanding bills—"

"I'm sure my lawyer will be able to convince you they are *your* responsibility." His voice had lost its congeniality.

Morgana studied the flowers strewn around her feet, crushing one under her heel in disgust. From the corner of her eye she saw the chimp climb over the crates and cages.

13

while stuffing himself with bananas. He was throwing the peels around the room.

"Mr. Wake, make no mistake. I'm a businesswoman. Your lawyer doesn't frighten me. You *will* receive an invoice for the unpaid portion of your wedding bill. I suggest you pay it promptly!" She slammed down the phone, barely missing her own fingers. "What *nerve!*"

Her adrenaline pumping like mad, Morgana turned to face the clutter. She was calculating her losses, trying to find a way to minimize them when the impact of the chimp's mischief hit her. Morgana closed her eyes to shut out the sight.

Knowing the mess would not disappear because she refused to look at it, Morgana reluctantly surveyed the damage. The chimp had strewn banana peels and mangoes around the room, but he hadn't done any real harm. At the moment he was on the highest stack of crates, trying to open a plastic jug.

"The piña colada mix. No, you don't." Morgana scolded him as she crossed the room to the devilish animal. "Come on, give it here," she coaxed.

Just out of her reach, the chimp seemed to delight in her efforts to take hold of him. He jumped up and down, screeching at her, then moved back and took the jug with him. While he renewed his efforts to open the bottle, Morgana pulled another crate next to his refuge. This time her long arms and legs couldn't do the trick alone.

"Be a nice boy, would you? I've had a hard day," she complained.

Morgana managed to get a grip on the bottle while the chimp succeeded in loosening the top. The struggle was short-lived. Morgana gave a huge tug. The chimp let go! It might have been an ocean wave approaching. Morgana saw it in slow motion. An undulating, rippling swell of whitish fluid separated into tiny splashing streams, missing her clothes by a scant few inches but spraying her face.

"Wait until I get my hands on you!" she threatened.

Jumping up and down on the box and pointing a finger at her, the chimp was making strange noises that sounded like laughter. Morgana lunged to grab him, but he scooted under the worktable. At that very moment she heard the door open and her sister Blanche's trilling voice.

"Step in here. Oh, dear, whatever are you up to, Morgana? You'll have to pardon the mess," Blanche said doubtfully to the couple who had followed her into the workroom. "Wait right here, won't you?" She rushed to Morgana.

Looking past her sister, Morgana stared into the cool gray eyes of a striking-looking man in a three-piece suit. Although she disliked the formal business attire intensely, Morgana had to admit he was elegantly dressed, the gray suit perfectly tailored to his tall, trim form. An Italian import no doubt. His companion was a young petite blonde casually dressed in a flame-colored Gibson girl blouse and turquoise jodhpur pants. Morgana thought they made a strange couple.

"What in the world has happened, Morgana?" Blanche's hazel eyes were wide with horror. "How embarrassing!" Blanche put on her best older-sister act and glared up at Morgana. "To think that this is what prospective clients are treated to on their very first visit!"

"Thank goodness you're here! I need help cleaning up this mess," Morgana said.

Blanche cringed. "In these clothes?" She looked down at her own typical work clothes—a pale lavender suit and white silk blouse. "Besides, I just did my nails."

Morgana should have known better than to suggest that

Blanche help. She sighed, wondering how she ever let her sister talk her into the wedding consultant business. All she wanted to do was design the gowns and accessories, but somehow it seemed she did most of the work.

"Blanche, I can't take care of all this alone," Morgana pleaded.

"Let Barney do it," Blanche insisted, referring to their only permanent—if semireliable—employee. "He said he would be here today."

"At two. He was going to help with the deliveries and inventory. It's almost four thirty now."

"If I'm late one more time, Terry will refuse to see me again!"

Morgana studied her sister's perfectly coiffed head. "You're leaving me with all this to get your hair done?"

"Yes, of course, dear," Blanche answered, patting the dark brown waves. "Evan and I have a dinner engagement this evening with his business associates. It's imperative I look my best."

"But, Blanche—"

"Now don't argue with me, Morgana. I want to introduce you to our new clients." Pausing for effect, she added, "They want us to do a medieval wedding!"

Was Morgana supposed to be thrilled by that news? Another far-out wedding wasn't something she felt equipped to deal with at the moment. Before she could protest, her sister was steering her toward the door, saying, "It will be quite a challenge since we have only five weeks to do it."

"Five weeks!" Morgana stopped dead in her tracks and glanced over at the couple, who seemed to be getting restless. The man was studying his watch. "Are you crazy, Blanche? No way!"

Blanche was aghast. "Morgana, don't you *dare* say such a

thing. Tomorrow a jungle wedding, next month a medieval. Think of the publicity!" Her eyes glittered as though she could envision scores of engaged couples lined up outside their door, demanding their very own fantasy weddings.

"The jungle wedding is off," Morgana whispered. "Canceled. They're eloping. To top it off, Wake doesn't want to settle his bill."

"What?" Blanche turned her sister aside, insisting, "We'll discuss this later, Morgana. I don't want to keep Mr. Bedford waiting one minute longer."

It seemed that Mr. Bedford was through with waiting, for when they turned back to their clients, the couple was approaching.

Morgana met the man's cool gaze again. He wasn't happy.

Blanche trilled nervously, "I want you to meet the creative force behind Fantasy Weddings. This"—she gestured dramatically, bravely trying to ignore her sister's dishevelment—"is my sister, Morgana Lawrence."

The young woman's expression was doubtful; the man's stare slightly hostile. Morgana flushed. The prospective groom was behaving rudely. The way he was inspecting her reminded Morgana of the banker she had dealt with in obtaining a loan to start their business. He hadn't approved of her either.

"This is Mariette DuMont"—Blanche faltered but shored herself up with a brave smile—"and Nicholas Bedford."

If his well-defined lips weren't in a straight, hard line, he would be handsome, Morgana thought. He had an interesting face, strong and angular, with a high forehead, long, straight nose, and square chin, enhanced by light brown hair styled to suit his features.

Ignoring his attitude, Morgana offered him her hand even

17

though it was slightly sticky from the piña colada mix. "Mr. Bedford." Morgana could have sworn his eyes softened in amusement as he felt the stickiness.

She turned to the young woman. "Miss DuMont."

"It seems we've caught you at a bad moment," Mariette said, smiling with genuine warmth. "Perhaps another day would be better for you."

"Oh, no. Don't concern yourself with *our* little internal problems." Blanche immediately assured her, not willing to let potential clients escape. "Morgana will be happy to take care of you, won't you, dear?" She swept by them toward the door.

Just then the phone rang. Blanche picked it up and turned to Morgana. "It's for you. A client."

"Blanche," Morgana said, taking the receiver, "why don't you take Miss DuMont and Mr. Bedford to the reception area and give them the sample books before you leave?"

"Of course," Blanche said, surprising Morgana. A brittle smile was plastered on her face. "After all," she said with a sniff, "I have nothing bettter to do with my time."

"Don't hurry, Miss Lawrence," Mariette said, her bright blue eyes as sincere as her smile. "We don't mind waiting."

Nicholas glanced at his watch again. *He* didn't seem to be the patient type.

"I won't be long," Morgana told them.

It took almost ten minutes to take care of the client on the phone. Morgana wished she had the time to fix herself up, but she didn't want to make the couple in the other room wait any longer. Sighing, she headed for the reception area, wondering about the relationship between Nicholas and Mariette as she went. She could see why any man would be attracted to Mariette. She reminded Morgana of a curvaceous Kewpie doll. Even so, Morgana wondered what a seri-

18

ous businessman in his mid-thirties could have in common with a teen-ager.

It made her remember theater director Miles Lord and his infidelities. He had been the first man she had ever really loved, and he had used her. He had wanted not Morgana the woman but Morgana the costume designer, yet not enough to give up his teen-aged groupies. Because of her experience with him, Morgana had rarely dated since she and Blanche had turned their business into a full-time venture.

Not that she had trouble attracting men. Morgana realized her best and worst features blended into a pleasing whole. Too tall and slender to be voluptuous, she could wear her own most unusual designs. Her features might be thin, but her black hair fell gloriously thick from a slight widow's peak. She didn't care for her lips, which were slightly pointed, but her large pale blue eyes pleased her well enough. Using her natural instincts, Morgana had designed a highly individualized look for herself and rarely strayed from it. Ruefully she glanced down at the T-shirt and shorts and wished this had not been one of those exceptions.

Shrugging, she opened the door to the office/reception area. A high-pitched giggle was the first sound Morgana heard. She winced, then was surprised when Barney's voice answered in its usual boisterous style.

"I see the procession being headed by the bride and groom mounted on two snow-white palfreys." A stylish character actor, Barney would never use a word as mundane as "horses." He had a flair for staging and loved doing research for ideas to make their weddings realistic. He tended to go overboard sometimes—well, most of the time—but the customers loved him.

19

"It sounds wonderful!" Mariette exclaimed. "Don't you love it, Nicky?"

Nicky! Morgana stopped, thinking it was disgusting that a man in his thirties allowed himself to be saddled with a childish nickname.

"If *you* love it, Mari, that's all that matters," Nicholas said.

Unnoticed, Morgana glared at him before turning her attention to Barney. Dressed in his usual sweat shirt, paint-spattered work pants, and tennis shoes that had seen better days, Barney had placed a pith helmet on his graying red head, adding a walking stick and spotted leopard cravat to get into the *jungle* mood.

Only his animated personality separated him from one of the manikins displaying Morgana's creations. Regency and Edwardian gowns filled the large picture window. A groom's futuristic jump suit decorated a corner. Barney could be an example—in bad taste, of course—of the late sixties.

How incongruous he appeared in the carefully decorated blue- and terra-cotta-walled room with its old Persian rug in matching shades. Her clients sat on a dark blue modern couch with their backs to her. Nicholas idly thumbed through a large sample book on a modern glass table. Nothing seemed to catch his interest, for he never stopped really to *look* at a page any more than he listened to Barney's prose from a medieval play.

When Barney spotted Morgana, he crossed to her, exclaiming in his most theatrical manner, "Morgana, darling! My, you are looking gorgeous today." He hugged her, then kissed both her cheeks. "Yum," he said as he tasted the piña colada on her face. At her scathing look he held his tongue.

20

"I was entertaining our new clients while they waited for you," he said instead.

"Yes, darling, and I've been waiting for *you* all day," she responded, patting his cheek with a still-sticky hand.

Morgana and Barney had been good friends since their theater days, so she found it difficult to play the outraged boss even though she was annoyed with him.

From the corner of her eye she could see Mariette and Nicholas peering at them through the potted palm next to the couch. At least something had finally caught Nicholas's interest. He raised a silvery eyebrow and dropped his gaze. He scrutinized her long, bare legs.

Determined Nicholas wouldn't fluster her, Morgana regally swept by Barney and perched on a Victorian chair opposite her clients. "I hope Barney has kept you suitably entertained?"

"Oh, he has, Miss Lawrence," an eager Mariette responded.

"I like to have my clients tell me about their dream wedding as best they can," Morgana said. "Any ideas you have, pictures or preferences in clothing . . . anything."

"Morgana," Mariette began, her smile pure sunshine, "I'd like my wedding to be as authentic as you can make it. When I was a little girl, my older brother filled my head with tales of knights in shining armor saving beautiful maidens in distress. They would always marry them, of course, and ride off together on a beautiful white horse." She shared an intimate smile with Nicholas. "I thought it all so romantic then," Mariette went on. "When I began college, I hadn't rid myself of the fascination of the period. I majored in art history with a specialty in the medieval period. Literature, music, art. And my minor is medieval history."

21

Morgana studied the blonde with a new respect. There was more to her than met the ear, she thought, remembering Mariette's giggles. Perhaps Nicholas was a history professor who had fallen in love with his student. Suddenly Morgana realized their period research would need to be intense and their results detailed. *Thank goodness for Barney,* she thought. He would delight in being authentic.

"I never thought my dream could come true until Larry Matthews told us about your enterprise. Right, Nicky?"

Morgana knew that was her cue, but she hesitated to jump right in with Blanche-like enthusiasm.

"Yes. Larry Matthews said you're doing a splendid job on his wedding. He suggested you could do the same for us."

The Matthews' Victorian wedding would be one of their simpler creations, Morgana thought. There was no comparison between the two.

Mariette went on. "I want to be removed from the twentieth century altogether in a medieval world without cars, buses, paved streets, or high-rises." Her china blue eyes snapped with excitement. "Can you do it, Morgana? Can you give me a world with knights in shining armor?"

"It's a tall order," Morgana admitted reluctantly. She noticed Nicholas's smug smile. She could almost hear him say, "I knew you couldn't from the moment I walked in the door." She rose to the challenge. "I'll see what I can do."

Defiantly staring into gray eyes so much like silvery smoked glass, Morgana lost her sense of the present. She felt drawn to Nicholas as a swirling mist enveloped them.

Morgana shook the feeling away as Barney said, "I've got an inspiration!"

"What?"

"Merlin's Medieval Magic Faire." He beamed proudly, then, noticing the blank expressions around him, explained.

22

"It's an *authentic* medieval fair that opened last weekend. I have not yet had the time to check it out personally, but I know people—very fine actors," he amended, "who are working there."

Morgana's attention drifted from Barney long enough for her to notice Nicholas staring at her. Sights and sounds receded into a haze as she and Nicholas drew ever closer. For the moment they were no longer in a twentieth-century office in Evanston, Illinois, but were drawn deep into a timeless void. His lips tantalized her.

"The fair covers a somewhat mystical period of history," Barney told them, landing Morgana neatly in the present. "I understand there's a medieval town with eateries and craft shops."

Morgana flushed uncomfortably, embarrassed at her inappropriate thoughts. She forced herself to concentrate on Barney's words, but she had the strangest feeling that a pair of gray eyes was caressing her.

"Troubadours and magicians stroll the grounds to amuse the crowds. And several psychics and tarot and palm readers have set up booths," Barney finished.

"But what does that have to do with the wedding?" Mari demanded, tossing her blond curls in excitement.

"Ideas, my dear young woman. It will offer our palates a virtual feast of ideas!"

"And perhaps a site," Morgana mused, her mind on her work once more. "You did say you wanted to be removed from this century?" As Mari shook her head vigorously in agreement, Morgana continued. "I'll call the manager of the fair and see what he thinks of the idea. It sounds as though it would add the right atmosphere."

"Oh, Nicky, doesn't it sound wonderful!"

"Right. Absolutely wonderful," he droned.

23

Irritated by his tone and perfunctory smile, Morgana wanted to gnash her teeth. If Nicholas Bedford proved to be so unenthusiastic throughout the planning, they would have a bumpy road to the end of this wedding!

"If you like," Morgana suggested, trying to ignore him, "we all could go to the fair next Sunday to see what it has to offer."

"I'll try to get away from school next weekend, but I can't promise. Nicky will go with you, though. After all, he has final approval since he's paying for the wedding."

Nicholas pulled out his wallet and extracted a business card. It was very plain, but Morgana noted the fine-quality white stock. Careful that their fingers didn't touch, she took it from him. A quick glance upward assured her Nicholas noticed her awkwardness. There was a definite twinkle in his eyes, and one brow was raised. Not knowing where else to look, Morgana glanced at the card.

Printed in neat block letters was the company's name and number. "Bedford and Associates, Financial Consultants. Nicholas Bedford, Director." She had been right. He *was* a banker.

"Call me anytime during the week," he told her, warmth gentling his voice.

But he called her later that night. Morgana had been trying to fall asleep for an hour. It wasn't worry that was keeping her awake. Luckily Barney had been able to sell the fruit and flowers from the Wake wedding fiasco to the Polynesian Gardens Restaurant, and Barney had given her his solemn word he would take care of the chimp and birds in the morning.

What bothered her was the flight of fancy she'd indulged in earlier. Morgana wondered how she could have been so

24

foolish. Nicholas Bedford was soon to be a married man. He *was* attractive, but she didn't even care for his type. She was appalled that her imagination could have taken such an inappropriate turn.

When the phone rang, she instinctively knew it was Nicholas. She picked up the receiver only to have her intuition confirmed.

"This is Nicholas Bedford," she heard the voice on the other end say.

"Ah, yes?" she said curtly, wondering why he was calling so late.

"Meeting you was quite an experience." Was that meant to be sarcastic? she wondered. He added, "I haven't been able to forget your remarkable outfit all evening."

"Really, Mr. Bedford!"

"Call me Nicholas," he said quickly. "I didn't mean to offend you. But you'll have to admit it was the most extraordinary dress for a business meeting." Amusement warmed his voice.

What could she say to that? "Mr. Bedford, why exactly did you call?"

"I was wondering if you would be free for dinner Wednesday evening?"

"Mr. Bedford!" Morgana was shocked. He was an engaged man! "I don't date my clients, especially not men who—"

"I thought we could discuss your designs," he said smoothly, making her feel a bit foolish.

"My designs," she echoed in a small voice.

"Yes. I assume you'll have them started by Wednesday. I would like to see what you've done before they're finalized." When she still hesitated, he added, "I do have approval on everything."

25

How very businesslike. The man didn't even trust the designs to her. She should have known he would insist on interfering before she even had time to develop her ideas.

"Dinner on Wednesday will be fine then."

"I'll be looking forward to it."

As she hung up, Morgana tried to rid herself of the tension his insistence had caused in her. He was a banker type all right. He didn't understand the first thing about a creative profession.

Morgana sighed. Sensing that he'd be difficult every step of the way, she certainly wasn't looking forward to working with Nicholas Bedford.

26

CHAPTER TWO

"I don't believe this!"

Morgana was hunched over the office desk, frantically searching for the sketches she had completed that morning. She raked a few straggly hairs from her eyes, then slammed her hand flat on the desk.

"I know I left them right here." She silently cursed the person who had moved them. "The shelves!"

As she impatiently lifted a stack of folders on the shelf closest to her, Morgana felt a nail snap down to the quick. "Damn!" Frustrated and next to tears, she sucked her forefinger, tasting a drop of her own blood. It wasn't her day.

Because she was running late, her hair hadn't quite dried when she attempted to use a curling iron on it—something she rarely did—so the sophisticated style she'd decided to try was short of perfect. And now her manicure was ruined.

"Where are those sketches?" she asked the walls through gritted teeth as she removed the finger from her mouth.

Her day was quickly going from bad to worse. Morgana had worked alone on the Fargate-Johnson wedding. It had a twenties theme, and Blanche promised the bride and her six maids they all could have dresses covered with bugle beads. Morgana had spent most of the day looking, but no one sold prebeaded material. Now she would have to find several women with extraordinary skills to bead yards and yards of fabric. And trying to find an authentic twenties band hadn't been any more rewarding. Next she would have to dress up and be the flapper.

In the rush and shuffle of the day, the medieval sketches had disappeared. Although Blanche had been scheduled into the office for a few hours, Morgana hadn't seen her. Of course, they might have missed each other when Morgana had gone to the printer to deliver the invitation copy Blanche had forgotten about. Barney had been in and out a few times, but as usual he was nowhere to be found when she needed him. If he himself weren't missing, *he* might be able to shed some light on the situation.

"Nicholas Bedford will not be pleased!" Morgana mumbled to herself, ransacking every shelf in the office.

She so wanted to offset his first impression of her. Not knowing where they'd go for dinner, she'd played it safe by wearing a highly stylish but casual outfit. The rainbow-striped gauze sundress had a short-sleeved purple jacket with red trim. Red sandals and chunky jewelry added the perfect accents. Morgana was satisfied with her appearance —except for her hair. Now if only she could find those sketches before pulling it all out!

"Morgana, darling. I've thought of the most won-n-nderful idea for the medieval wedding." Barney made his usual dramatic entrance without any formal preliminaries such as a simple "hello." Decorating his sweat shirt was a red and gold crest with a magnificent lion. "You didn't seem too enthusiastic about the venison idea, so I did more research. What would you say to a procession of waiters carrying platters of food, led by a pickled boar's head!" His grin was triumphant.

Venting her day's irritation on him, Morgana snapped,

28

"No boar's head. Don't even mention it to our clients! Can't you *ever* think simple?" she demanded.

"Sorry," he said apologetically. "Things haven't been going too well today, have they?"

"I can't find the medieval sketches I finished this morning, and Nicholas Bedford is due any moment," Morgana complained to him.

"Have you looked in the files?"

"The files?" Morgana repeated.

"Yes. Isn't that what they're for? I did some straightening up earlier. I thought I'd help clean up this mess, so I put the sketches where I *thought* you'd want them." His hurt tone was sincere, Morgana knew, for Barney had his share of sensitivity, especially when he was trying to please someone.

"Oh, Barney . . ." Morgana didn't know what to say. She felt like a hot-air balloon too quickly deflated. Before she could apologize, she heard the outside door open. "The sketches!"

Morgana spun around to the files. She yanked out a drawer, catching her hose. A huge run spread from mid-shin to thigh. "Double damn!" she exclaimed just as Nicholas came into the office. Her hands fumbled with the folder, and the sketches flew to the floor. Barney scrambled to pick them up.

Nicholas grinned as he watched the flurry of activity. He was dressed to perfection, of course. His casual dinner jacket was of the darkest gray, set off by a snow-white shirt with dozens of tiny pleats. Morgana realized her dress was inappropriate after all.

"Mr. Bedford," she said as she crossed the few yards to the doorway. She gave him her hand before realizing it was the one with the broken nail. An unruly lock of hair chose that very moment to fall across her eyes.

29

Morgana brushed the hair from her forehead as Barney slipped the folder into a smart leather case and handed it to her.

"Here you are, love."

"Are you ready to leave?" Nicholas asked.

"I didn't realize you would want to go formal."

"I thought you might enjoy dinner at the Pump Room, but we could eat anywhere you like."

"The Pump Room will be fine. Give me a moment to put on something a little fancier. I live right here, so I won't be long."

"Need any help?" he asked. His comment sounded like a come-on, but when it was combined with his straight face and businesslike demeanor, Morgana wasn't positive.

"No, really, I'll be right back."

Entering the Pump Room an hour later, Morgana was uncertain about her second choice. She had dressed in one of her favorites, a knee-length black silk, draped in the front and practically backless. Nicholas kept his hand on the small of her back past the myriad autographed pictures of celebrities lining the entryway walls and the enormous wooden bar crowded with well-suited men and sleek women. Vainly Morgana tried to ignore the ripple of sensation that traveled up and down her spine. They followed the maître d' down into the restaurant area. Its soft-lit neutral decor lent a subtle elegance to the atmosphere. Morgana was relieved when they slipped into their sculptured gray booth.

Immediately a tuxedoed waiter appeared to take their cocktail order. Nicholas and Morgana agreed on a bottle of Moselle wine instead of mixed drinks.

Since this was a business dinner, Morgana reached for her

leather case and slipped out the folder. "I think you'll be pleased with my designs."

He laid his hand over hers, stopping her from showing him. "Later. Let's enjoy our wine and have a relaxing dinner before we descend to the mundane."

"My designs are anything but mundane," Morgana answered a bit angrily, freeing her hand. How dare he insult her work! "Take a look at this!" she demanded, practically shoving one under his nose. "If you want the mundane, you've come to the wrong person."

"I didn't mean your designs were mundane," he said. He held her eyes with his own. "I meant we don't need to discuss *business* right now. I'll look at those later."

He hadn't even glanced down at the sketch when the wine arrived. Nicholas tasted it and gave the waiter his nod of approval.

"We'd like to order now."

A waitress in a black, skirted tux brought the menus and expanded on the selections with the chef's daily specials before leaving them to decide.

Over her wineglass Morgana stole surreptitious glances at her dinner partner while looking at the entrées on the menu. When *were* they supposed to get down to business? she wondered. If he didn't want to see the sketches, what could they talk about? After the waitress had taken their orders, they drank their wine in a surprisingly comfortable silence.

Once more Morgana noticed Nicholas was certainly easy on the eyes. In the dim light the candle flames picked out the fine streaks of silver at his temples and matching silver flecks in his gray eyes. Shaking herself from such personal observations, Morgana decided to resume the conversation about the wedding.

"I called the manager of the fair yesterday. He's willing to

31

discuss our using the grounds for the wedding. We can take a look at the place on Sunday, but he won't be there."

"Ah, here come the appetizers," Nicholas said, changing the subject. Obviously he wouldn't be swayed to talk business until after dinner.

Conversing with Nicholas Bedford was not as difficult as Morgana had feared. Although he didn't probe too deeply into anything political, he shared several amusing anecdotes about the present administration to get them through the escargots. While they ate their spinach salad, he made conventional small talk. She found herself thinking that it was the kind of conversation people make on a first date. How ridiculous that she should think such a thing! By the time the main course of medallions of veal arrived, he had maneuvered the conversation to her.

"I'm sure you didn't start out designing unique wedding fashions. What did you do before you went into business with your sister?"

"I went from designing children's togs to uniforms while I was in New York. All the uninspiring fashions most designers have to start with," she said, chuckling. He grinned in response. "I was homesick as well as bored, so I came back to Chicago. A friend from the Art Institute was designing sets for various theater groups, and she remembered I loved costuming. She recommended my work to a theater director who was doing a historical play. That's when my career really began."

"I would think there's money to be made in costuming."

"Sometimes there is," she said softly. His question had awakened unpleasant memories. Miles Lord had made sure Morgana had not received adequate compensation for her work. The director had cheated her financially as well as emotionally. She was almost ready to explain what had happened to her, but when she looked into the face of her dinner partner, she was brought back to reality—and the present. She was not about to tell Nicholas Bedford about Miles!

Instead, she answered, "Oh, you can make money in New York or even in other major theaters here, but those jobs are few and far between. The Milestone was having financial difficulties when I was hired. I had to work as a temporary secretary once in a while. Then, too, my designs were subject to the whims of the director, but costuming *was* interesting. It gave me an excellent background for my own business."

Morgana wondered why she had almost shared such personal memories with a client. Because Nicholas had put her at ease so completely, they hadn't broached the subject of the wedding, and her designs were still in the folder, unseen.

Determined to force them on him, if necessary, Morgana laid the folder down on the table as soon as the waiter took away their dessert plates.

"Why don't we start with the bride's gown?" she suggested assertively.

Nicholas raised an eyebrow but took the sketches from her. To Morgana's irritation he merely glanced at the designs and made perfunctory comments about them. "These look fine. I'm sure Mariette will be pleased when she sees them," he said absently, slipping them back into the folder.

"Mr. Bedford, there happen to be several variations in the sketches. I thought you wanted some say in the final designs."

"They're all fine." He reached for the sketches once more, adding, "My name is Nicholas." He made a pretense of reexamining them, but Morgana was sure he didn't look at them any more closely than the first time. "Any one will do."

33

Morgana was angry at his offhand attitude. She'd put in extra time and special effort to give him some choices, and he acted as though he wanted to get the approvals done with as quickly as possible. Then *why* had he arranged this "business" dinner?

A growing suspicion took seed, making Morgana apprehensive. In addition to avoiding business all evening, he had indulged in small talk, leading to personal questions about her personal life! Could it be he was making a play for her? He might be one of those men so confident of their own charm that they couldn't imagine a woman not wanting them. What did it matter if he was available or not? She'd met that type before!

Morgana was annoyed as she put away the sketches, wondering if she should even bother taking out the others.

"How would you like to work off some of the calories we've consumed?" he asked. Morgana blinked rapidly, now extremely wary of him. "On the dance floor," he added most innocently.

Wondering if she should refuse graciously and insist they finish discussing business, Morgana hesitated. Business deals were sealed on golf courses and tennis courts every day, an inner voice reasoned, so why not on a dance floor? She could control herself, Morgana thought. She rose and offered Nicholas her hand.

He led her to the tiny dance floor and there pulled her close so the length of her body touched his lightly at every point. His nearness made her uncomfortable, but the piano's magic relaxed her until she floated in his arms. Lost in the music, Morgana closed her eyes and created visions for herself such as those the sentimental words invoked. Nicholas's suggestive murmuring dispelled them.

"I like the way you move." His breath nuzzled the fine

hairs around her face. She pulled back determinedly, then felt his hand pressing into the exposed small of her back. His warmth surrounded her.

Aware of each finger's length and texture, Morgana said lightly, "Thanks for the compliment. But I'm a little rusty." As Nicholas fanned his fingers across her spine, she drew in a deep breath. Her nostrils filled with his pleasant masculine scent.

"Come now. Don't tell me no one takes you dancing?"

"When I work twelve-hour days, I don't have the energy," she said weakly, wondering how to regain control of the situation. She was dancing with a client, not a lover, for heaven's sake! Next time she'd stick to the tennis courts to do business with him.

"Really? Twelve-hour days?" He seemed amused. "You *really* devote so much time to a frivolous venture?"

Morgana felt her temper flare. *Another* criticism of her work! Nicholas Bedford didn't respect her profession. Obviously, to him, a "frivolous venture" such as Fantasy Weddings could never require that kind of time. Not wanting to lose a lucrative business deal, Morgana forced herself to shrug off the question with a "frivolous" reply. "It's the consuming passion in my life. As a matter of fact, I feel an uncontrollable urge to get back to work!"

Although the music hadn't ended, Morgana stomped off the dance floor, leaving Nicholas no choice but to follow.

By the time he joined her at the table, she'd whipped out the remaining sketches. He eyed them as he slid closer to her.

"Here are the rest of my designs," she told him in her most businesslike voice. "Will you pick the ones to use, or shall I?"

"Show me your favorites," Nicholas suggested. His expression was serious except for the glint in his eyes.

Knowing he was enjoying himself—could he actually be toying with her? she wondered—Morgana was further irritated. Shuffling through her sketches, she pulled out what she thought to be a winning hand. Aggressively she slapped them down in front of him.

Staring Nicholas straight in the eye, she demanded, "Tell me what you think."

She could have sworn he tempered the urge to smile before looking down at the sketches. He really seemed to be studying them when he murmured, *"I think* your work becomes you. It *does* turn you on. Rather nicely, if I may say so."

As he raised his eyes to hers, Morgana flushed. There was no mistaking the desire she read in their smoky depths. She fought their enticing lure.

"Then you approve?" she asked, controlling her voice, quickly adding, "The designs?" so there would be no mistaking her meaning.

"I certainly do approve," he said, still staring at her. Then he, too, added quite deliberately, "The designs."

An awkward silence hung between them for what seemed like an eternity before their waitress interrupted. "Can I get you anything else?"

"The check," Nicholas told her without dropping his gaze from Morgana's face.

Morgana sizzled as she collected her designs, deposited them in the folder, and stuck it in the briefcase. He *was* making a play for her, and she didn't know how to handle it without embarrassing herself. And if she lost the account, Blanche would be livid. Silence seemed her safest weapon.

Nicholas didn't seem eager to challenge her again. He

said nothing more than necessary to start them on the road home. Morgana entered his silver gray sedan with gratitude. She rested tensely against the custom black interior, then closed her eyes and tried to shut off her mind as they sped north on Lake Shore Drive.

She jumped when she felt his hand on her knee. Appalled, she stared down at it as he said, "I'll have to thank Larry Matthews for telling me about Fantasy Weddings." His fingers traced a light pattern through the silk material. "Do you get many recommendations?" he asked, his voice low and husky.

The question sounded more personal than professional, but Morgana let it go. Deftly she slipped her leg from his touch and crossed it. He put his hand back on the steering wheel.

"Actually I do get quite a few *referrals,*" Morgana told him in what she hoped was a normal voice. Her knee tingled in the most exasperating way! "Usually not until after the wedding, however. Larry Matthews isn't getting married for another two weeks."

"I know."

She was thankful that they were only a few blocks from her building. They couldn't get there fast enough for Morgana.

"Larry told me he's highly satisfied with your services."

Was she imagining it, or did many of his casually issued statements have deeper meanings?

Trying to steer the conversation in a safe direction, she asked, "Is Mr. Matthews a business acquaintance or a personal friend?" Only one block to go.

"He's both."

Nicholas didn't say another word until they pulled up in front of her apartment. The second the car pulled to a stop,

37

he leaned closer to Morgana. "You know, when there's no written contract involved, it's customary to seal a verbal agreement."

Her heart began to thud erratically. "Yes, I believe a handshake is in order." She held out her hand.

He took it, but in an intimate way, and brought it to his chest as he murmured, "I have a more personal gesture in mind."

Nicholas slipped his right arm around her shoulders and pulled her to him. Horrified, Morgana told her dazed mind to do something as his play for her turned into a pass.

"Nicholas," she said, meaning to stop him. If only she hadn't been able to see his eyes.

Even in the darkened car she could see the spun silver threads that drew her to him. His lips found hers, forcing her back over the threshold of time, suspending the present. There was no Mariette, no wedding to consider, only tender emotions spanning centuries.

Had his lips been demanding rather than seeking, she might have been able to save herself, but their very gentleness seduced her farther from the present. His tongue was exquisitely tender as it explored her mouth, seeking her magic, asking for her response. She couldn't resist its lure. For the moment Morgana let herself feel.

Pent-up emotions she'd buried deep inside were released in that brief yet seemingly endless kiss. Part of her questioned her willingness to bestow tenderness, affection, passion, and all the other feelings she had repressed for so long on a stranger. Yet another part of her knew this man, who sought her pleasure so gently, as if they had been partners through eternity. Morgana needed more than emotion. She needed to touch him.

Her hand found the side of his face and slipped up to

stroke his hair. Its silver was not cold like metal, but warm and vibrant just like the man. When she slipped her hand lower and rubbed her fingertips against the short hairs at the back of his neck, he gasped with pleasure and drew away.

"Morgana," he whispered, "you really are a woman of many talents. I'll be looking forward to discovering more of them working on the wedding together."

The wedding! Morgana snapped back to the present, feeling terribly humiliated when she realized she'd been madly embracing a client. A prospective groom no less! What kind of man was he?

"The only talents *you'll* get to explore will be my professional ones!" Morgana hissed, angrily pushing him away. She fumbled for her briefcase.

"I don't understand."

He actually had the nerve to sound offended!

"Can you deny you've treated the entire evening like a first date? Or that you were more interested in looking *me* over than you were in my designs?"

"No. Why should I deny it?"

"Oh!" Morgana reached for the door handle. He caught her arm, but she shook it off. "Tell *that* to Mariette and see what *she* thinks about it!"

"Why should she care?" he asked as she opened the door and slid out. "Our relationship has nothing to do with her!" he said huffily.

Now he had the nerve to be angry!

Morgana slammed the car door and stalked away. She was furious with him. How dare he think her the kind of woman who would welcome the advances of a soon-to-be married man!

"Morgana, wait a minute!" he commanded, stepping out of his car.

She fumbled with her key but got the door open. "Good night, *Mr. Bedford!*"

"Nicholas!" he shouted.

She slammed that door closed for good measure. A few seconds later she heard his car take off as though he had floored it.

"Damn!" she muttered, furious with herself.

Knowing she couldn't sleep, being as angry as she was, Morgana didn't even bother to climb the stairs to her apartment. Instead, she headed for the office, knowing she could calm down by concentrating on work.

Still seething, Morgana entered the office and flipped on the light. One look at the desk, and she knew Blanche had been there. Papers were strewn all over.

Near tears, she groaned out loud. "Oh, Blanche, why do you do this to me?"

Morgana sorted through the papers and stopped when she found the envelope marked "BEDFORD/DUMONT" in her sister's bold scrawl. Inside was the copy for Nicholas and Mari's wedding invitation. Feeling masochistic, she read it. And as she did, her pale blue eyes flew open in astonishment.

"*Who* is Christopher Paige?" she said aloud.

Shaking her head, she read it again.

"Mr. Nicholas Bedford is proud to invite you to attend the marriage of his sister Mariette DuMont to Christopher Paige, son of—"

Confused, she stared off into the distance. "He's not getting married? But why didn't he tell me?" Morgana repeated it, but with a different emphasis. "He's not getting married!"

Then, ever so slowly, a smile curled her lips. Morgana dropped the invitation information on the desk. After slipping off her evening sandals, she leaned back in her chair, propped her feet up on the desk, and laughed. Would he overlook her crazy behavior? She hoped so.

Planning the medieval wedding might be a pleasant experience after all.

41

CHAPTER THREE

The late-morning sun glinted on the castlelike walls surrounding the grounds of Merlin's Medieval Magic Faire. The clear golden light penetrated the surrounding wooded area so that filtered, glowing shafts found their way to the earthen floor.

Waiting in line to buy tickets, Morgana became fascinated by the color of Nicholas's hair. The sun transformed its light brown to a burnished gold, and with its silver highlights, she could fancy him a knight of olden times.

Morgana chuckled. Her imagination was always working. She hoped she'd use it to put together the details of the medieval wedding before the end of the day. If only the fair didn't get too crowded. Morgana surveyed the growing ticket line. She didn't look forward to wading through hordes of people on a hot and humid day.

She turned to ask Nicholas a question and found herself jostled into him. The line was suddenly moving.

"Sorry," she mumbled, one palm against his chest.

"No problem," Nicholas said casually. He steadied her with firm hands.

Her cheeks burning, Morgana turned and moved with the crowd. How could the man keep his composure so well? He hadn't said a thing about their dinner meeting. He acted as if his pass and her angry outburst had never happened. But then, Morgana decided, perhaps it was better that way. She shouldn't get personally involved with a client. He wasn't her type anyway.

The crowd pressed forward, surging past the ticket booth and over a small drawbridge. Morgana found herself deposited near a gravel path, Nicholas beside her.

The reedy melody of a distant flute cut through the murmurs of the spreading groups of people. Morgana could smell incense and the odor of cooking food. Looking down the path, she saw it led past booths displaying various merchandise. The small structures had been built to resemble medieval houses, with korbeled false second stories and fronts that lowered on hinges to display wares.

"It's too bad Mariette couldn't come today," Morgana said. "I'd like her to see the fair if we think it would make a good site for the wedding."

"She trusts me to assess the value of your ideas."

"But Mariette has a genuine interest in the medieval. I would think you'd find the wedding's financial details more in *your* line."

Morgana remembered the perfunctory glances Nicholas had given her costume sketches.

"I'll struggle along."

Nicholas seemed so sincere that Morgana smiled. He looked and acted relaxed. Since she would be alone with him for the day, Morgana needed to feel comfortable. Barney wouldn't be around. After parking his decrepit van in the fair's lot, he'd pointed out the entry gate to Morgana, then disappeared with some of his crazy actor friends.

"Let's explore." Morgana led the way. With a twirl of her purple and green striped skirt, she headed toward a booth featuring rentable costume clothing. Soon she was examining cheaply sewn tunics and trying on hats. She discarded a

43

feathered one and placed a magenta conelike headdress on her dark hair.

"This is a hennin—a medieval woman's hat," she explained to Nicholas. "I can't see what it looks like."

Morgana scowled into a small mirror on the counter. Turn and try as she might, she was unable to see the top of the two-foot-tall headpiece.

"It's very becoming," murmured Nicholas, close at her side. "Are you going to buy it?"

"What?" Morgana gave up her struggle with the mirror and threw down the hennin. "I don't want to buy anything. I just like to look. I get ideas."

"I'm getting ideas, too."

Morgana caught her breath. Was he back to making innuendos? She forced herself to frown because she didn't want him to think that she was interested.

"Why don't *you* try on some hats? It'll get you into the medieval mood." She picked up a sample. "Here. Try this black velvet one with the *turkey* feather."

Complying, Nicholas set the soft, floppy hat at an angle on his head. They both leaned forward to peer into the mirror.

"Not bad," said Nicholas, raising his eyebrows at her. "Now I'm getting into the *mood.*" His tone was intimate.

"You'll need a sword, too," said Morgana quickly as she straightened up. "No self-respecting nobleman would be without a weapon." She rummaged through a pile of plastic swords at the other end of the counter and finally chose one decorated with fake jewels.

Nicholas took the toy and made a few experimental jabs in the air. Grinning, he replaced it on the counter and removed the hat. "I don't think these props are my style. I'm

44

the sort who needs well-tailored outfits. You know, the classic three-piece armor look."

Morgana joined his laughter. She had to admire his sarcastic wit.

"This is really fun," he said, then gestured broadly at the spectacle around them. "Shall we have some more?"

Morgana took the arm he offered as they walked down the path. "I see you *do* dress casually at times," she said, referring to the clothing he was wearing—an open-necked blue shirt and gray sports pants.

"On appropriate occasions," he agreed. "Is that a costume you're wearing? It's beautiful."

As she turned to him, Morgana realized he was staring at the low-cut neckline of her laced-up bodice.

"I've always liked this medieval peasant look," Morgana managed to say casually, while nervously smoothing her full medium-length skirt. "There's a cotton batiste undertunic that goes with it, but it was too humid to wear a second layer." Morgana flushed. Why was she telling him about undergarments she hadn't worn? "I designed it for the opening party of *Camelot* when I was with the Milestone Theater." She rushed on to add, "They really did combine odd colors like purple and green in the Middle Ages, you know."

"I don't doubt your word. Tell me, what did medieval ladies wear *under* their undertunics?" His eyes seemed to have roamed to her bodice once again.

"You'll have to ask Barney." Morgana's breasts tingled. "He's the expert on historical detail."

"He's an expert on underwear?"

"Barney's a specialist concerning all *kinds* of historical facts." Changing the subject, she pointed. "Look, there's a performance going on."

Grabbing his arm, Morgana towed Nicholas past a stall

45

selling fresh flower garlands and a booth advertising face painting to a wooden platform erected near the fair's outer wall. Several actors dressed as Sherwood Forest outlaws were sitting on the stage watching two girls perform a dance to flute and drum.

Releasing Nicholas's arm, Morgana opened her shoulder bag to take out a notebook and pen. She scribbled rapidly.

"Getting ideas for the wedding?" he asked her.

"Wouldn't dancers be nice? Mariette agreed that strolling entertainers could add an authentic touch."

When Nicholas didn't reply, she replaced her notebook and Morgana moved away. Nicholas followed, and they skirted the stage, following the winding path as it curved more deeply into the central area of the woods. More booths, their counters displaying products made by local artisans and artists, edged the path. Jewelry, leather goods, pottery, and stained glass surrounded them.

"Look at this booth, Morgana. How would you like a magic wand to make your fantasies come true?" It was a tempting offer. Too bad it wouldn't really work, Morgana thought. "Or how about a silver necklace of stars and moons?" He held an unusual piece of jewelry against her. "It suits you."

Before she could protest, he fastened it around her neck and pulled out his wallet and bought it for her. She was so dazed by the unexpected gesture she didn't even inspect the key chains, astrological charms, and other magical goods. After thanking him, she found something else to interest her.

"Look at the small tents over there. Aren't they charming?" Morgana had noticed the colorful tents and canopies set among many of the buildings. "Let's go find out how to

46

slay the dragon," she suggested, leading the way to a larger green canopy.

A throw of the bones decided how many spears a game player could aim at the red and green dragon painted on the backboard. If a spear landed in a hole—one of the dragon's spots—it earned points, eventually entitling the player to win a prize.

"Let's try it," Morgana said coaxingly. Throwing the lightweight spears looked easy. "Why don't you toss the bones, Nicholas?"

Taking the objects from her, he threw them with an off-hand gesture.

"Six tries at the dragon!" the game master announced, handing them six spears.

"I haven't done anything like this in a long time," Nicholas protested when Morgana urged him to go first. Nevertheless, he hefted a small spear and sent it sailing into one of the spots.

"Twenty points!" yelled the game master. "Eighty more for a prize."

The next two throws yielded another fifty. Nicholas displayed a self-satisfied grin as he turned to Morgana. "Not too bad for a rusty knight. Now it's milady's turn."

Morgana picked up a spear and attempted to assume the graceful pose Nicholas had used, but it was not as easy as it looked. Her first spear bounced awkwardly off the ground, far in front of the wooden dragon.

"Careful, fair maiden!" the game master yelled. "Don't kill any of the spectators!"

Morgana's face burned. Nicholas was standing right behind her. "I think you need to hold your shoulder farther back," he instructed, positioning himself more closely against her. His long fingers closed around Morgana's fore-

47

arm as he helped her wield a spear above her shoulder. His breath warmed the side of her throat. "I think your bodice may be laced too tight. It hampers the movement of your arm." Their eyes met for a second, before his traveled down to the deep purple lacings between her breasts.

Morgana thought her heartbeat must be visible through her cotton dress. She could feel Nicholas's heartbeat in return, thudding against her left shoulder blade. The entire front of his torso touched the length of her back.

"Um," Morgana stammered, "I guess I'm not dressed for this. Why don't you finish for me?"

Nicholas let her go reluctantly. She realized they were providing a show for the other game players.

"I thought you were the one who wanted to play this game?" he teased.

The slight wind cooled Morgana's heated body. She was surprised at the depth of her attraction to Nicholas Bedford. It was disconcerting, to say the least.

Nicholas picked up the key chain he had won. Proudly he dangled the little metal dragon before her. "For you, milady."

"You are too kind, sir knight. I have this wondrous necklace to remember the fair by. If you give me that, you will have naught. I beg you to keep it."

"Ah, but, fair lady, there is a much greater prize I'd be delighted to claim."

Morgana's pulse surged as she noted his smug smile. He was at it again, she thought, but this time she would let herself enjoy his understated humor.

They ambled on down the road. Nicholas paused at a booth marked "Heraldry." "These are fantastic!" he exclaimed.

Morgana gazed at the rows of plaques—representations of shields decorated with animals and symbols.

"Aren't these colors great?" Nicholas picked up a plaque to admire it.

Seeing him with the shield, Morgana could imagine him as a gold and silver knight. He walked with grace, yet there was strength in his movement. He was clever and intelligent and possessed a good sense of humor. As she admired his clear-cut profile, Morgana was sure the ladies would swoon for the Bedford knight.

"Red, blue, black, green, and purple," Nicholas continued. "Those are the true colors of heraldry. The lions are nicely executed, too. They were the most popular symbols."

"How is it you know so much about heraldry? I thought you knew nothing about the Middle Ages."

"I didn't say that. When I was a kid, I used to love the King Arthur and the Knights of the Round Table legend. I read everything I could about heraldry. I even sent away for the Bedford family shield."

"Why did you let me continue to explain everything?" she accused.

"I'm no expert. Besides, I enjoy listening to your descriptions."

Morgana didn't know whether to be offended or embarrassed. Suddenly things clicked into place. "You're the older brother! The one who told Mariette stories of knights in shining armor!" She glared at Nicholas as though he had intentionally withheld that information.

"Of course I am." Nicholas chuckled. "Who did you think she was talking about? She's got only one brother."

Morgana wasn't going to touch that one, even though she was curious about their different last names. Mistaking

Nicholas for the groom was embarrassing enough without telling him about it.

"Alms? Please, kind lady or sir. Some coins for the poor?" A couple of ragged beggars with wild hair and blackened teeth interrupted their conversation.

The sleazy-looking woman circled a startled Nicholas. "Or maybe ye'll dance with me, handsome gentleman?"

Morgana laughed at the strolling actors and jumped as the man grabbed the hem of her skirt. Grinning, Nicholas flipped them a coin. "We'll dance later," he said.

Watching his animated face and having experienced his unexpected enthusiasm, Morgana realized Nicholas had a complex personality. He could be cool and aloof but had warmth when he chose. Obviously an astute businessman, he had interests beyond ledgers and figures. His unpredictability made him intriguing and a bit of a mystery. Since Morgana had always loved mysteries, she was anxious to penetrate farther beneath his sophisticated exterior.

Now that they had reached the center of the fair, the crowd had thinned. Morgana was pleased with the ambience supplied by the colorful costumed actors who peopled the medieval world and by the sound of a stringed instrument, probably a lute, repeating a circling melody. She danced down the pathway, making up steps as she went. Nicholas grinned as she did a complicated turn in front of him.

Located in the center of the fair's circular grounds, the refreshment area housed a dozen canopies. The first booth advertised an authentic medieval drink.

"Mead. I've never seen that for sale before. Come on," Nicholas insisted. He purchased two large paper cups filled with the ale flavored with honey and spices.

The pleasantly sweet liquid slid down Morgana's throat. "M-m-m. It *is* nice."

She noticed a gathering near the flat top of a small knoll. King Arthur, Merlin, the magician, and Arthur's sorceress half sister Morgan le Fay held court. The actress playing Morgan had a vibrant, husky voice. "A curse on you, Arthur! Merlin is old. His powers cannot protect you forever!"

Although Morgana watched the play attentively, she noticed when Nicholas slipped his arm around her waist. Yet her focus didn't shift to him completely. He drew her closer, his fingers finding her upper arm and caressing the bare skin. Her creativity humming, Morgana took out her notebook, trying to balance it and her cup of mead.

"Wouldn't it be interesting to have a character—an actress—like Morgan le Fay telling fortunes at the wedding?" she asked Nicholas. "She could read runes or cards."

Ignoring his silence, Morgana turned, extricating herself from his grasp. She looked over the refreshment canopies and jotted in her book. "We can have a wedding pavilion with canopies erected along the edge of the forest. We can have a refreshment pavilion, too. Wouldn't that be beautiful in a natural setting?" she asked enthusiastically. "And after the wedding feast the guests could join the fair's activities. Maybe Barney's palfreys would even be possible!"

She waited for Nicholas to share in her excitement.

Instead, a frown creased his brow. "Don't you ever think about anything but work? Oh, but I forgot, you're the woman who works twelve-hour days."

His flippancy bothered Morgana. It reminded her of his "frivolous venture" remark that had set her off the other night. In addition, Nicholas was supposed to approve her ideas. A little difficult when he wouldn't even discuss them, she thought.

"By the way, where's Barney?" Nicholas demanded. "Off somewhere writing in *his* notebook?"

51

"Barney's a walking encyclopedia," an annoyed Morgana told him. "He doesn't need to write everything down."

"If he did, you might have more time to enjoy yourself."

"This *is* a business outing," Morgana said to remind him. They both were silent for a moment.

"You *do* eat when you work, don't you?" Nicholas ventured carefully. He gazed at the refreshment area wistfully.

Sighing, Morgana decided to make the best of things and to enjoy his company for the rest of the day. Confident in her ideas for the wedding, Morgana was sure Mariette would approve, even if Nicholas didn't.

"Sure," Morgana said. "I'm ravenous."

They approached the open barbecue pits, where chickens, ribs, and huge turkey drumsticks roasted.

"M-m-m-m. Delicious!" Morgana smelled the tantalizing odor. "I'll try the chicken."

"Me, too." Nicholas bought two paper baskets, each loaded with half a chicken, broasted potatoes, and steaming corn on the cob. "I can't resist. I'm going to get a turkey leg, too."

Morgana checked out the rustic picnic tables located to one side of the cooking area, but there was no room to sit down.

"Standing room only," she told Nicholas when he approached her, his arms full.

"Let's walk over there. Maybe we can find a less inhabited place for a picnic."

"Sure. Let me help you carry some of that."

She took the jug of mead and walked beside him, swinging it, then reached inside a basket Nicholas was carrying and secured a sliver of chicken breast.

"Hey! What about me?" demanded Nicholas. Morgana obligingly tore off some chicken and popped a tidbit into his mouth. "Thanks," he mumbled. Before she could withdraw her hand, he licked her fingers. "Wouldn't want you to get food stains on your dress," he remarked wickedly.

Passing a sign that read "To the Palfreys" with an arrow pointing down a shady, quiet path, they decided to follow it.

"Why don't we eat down there?" She motioned toward a copse of trees down the bank.

In agreement, Nicholas carefully edged his way down the steep slope, Morgana right behind him. She was glad she had worn her flat-soled sandals. They came to a clearing in the trees, where Nicholas set the basket down. "Isn't this beautiful?" Morgana loved the way small patches of sky peeked through the tops of broadleaf and pine trees that surrounded them, forming a natural shelter. Shafts of light pierced the green canopy, giving the clearing a soft glow. A scent of soil and pine filled the air.

Morgana lowered herself to the grass carpet and ran her fingers over the green tendrils. "It's too bad we don't have a blanket, but the grass is dry," she said, pulling the combs from her hair, letting it swirl around her head wildly.

Nicholas set out the baskets and napkins, then laid out the food. They devoured the chicken and potatoes. It was strangely quiet in the small clearing. The raucous noises and frantic activities of the fair receded into the distance.

"Were you named for Morgan le Fay?" Nicholas asked.

Knowing he was referring to Arthur's sorceress, Morgana said, "I don't think so. My mother was an English teacher, but I don't remember her mentioning Morgan le Fay. I don't think I'd care to be named for an evil character."

Still chewing his food, Nicholas went on. "I remember reading somewhere that Morgan was ill used by the Arthurian legends. She originated in much older myths, you know. Often she was portrayed as an evil witch just because

53

she had supernatural powers, but I prefer to think of Morgan le Fay as a great enchantress."

"A truly romantic notion." Morgana approved. He had surprised her again. She sank onto one elbow, tipping back her head to peer at the treetops. Her long hair fanned out behind her, the ends nearly touching the grass.

Nicholas moved closer and touched the silky strands wonderingly. "You look like an enchantress now," he whispered, "with your black hair loose around your face." He ran one finger across her cheekbone and traced a line down the curve of her throat. As he rested his hand lightly on her shoulder, Morgana leaned back farther. Nicholas's face was so close. She met his searching silver gaze. Those eyes—they attracted and entangled.

"I think you're the sorcerer," Morgana whispered.

Nicholas pulled Morgana onto the grass with him. Her hair spread around her face, framing it. As Nicholas leaned over her, she smelled the scent of mead on his warm breath. His strong hands caressed her back and drew her closer. Morgana unconsciously responded, arching against him. His lips sought hers, gently at first, but then his kiss bruised her mouth, hard teeth against teeth. His inquiring, invading tongue entered the moist cave of her mouth and explored it. Morgana's long-dormant passions were summoned from deep within her by a modern-day magician.

In the quiet center of a medieval forest, a primeval green paradise, she was being loved by a sorcerer of extraordinary powers whose lips tasted of mead and were even more intoxicating than the potent drink. They were no longer in the present. Time lost all meaning. Centuries receded as her hands kneaded Nicholas's strong back and she felt his body's warmth pulsing from beneath his shirt. Under his spell completely now, she was unaware of the exact moment her hands sought the feel of his flesh. Their touch inspired him to new daring.

Tenderly nipping her lips with his teeth, Nicholas deftly loosened the lacings of her bodice. His fingers caressed the waiting flesh beneath. Her strapless bra was no barrier for his exploring fingers. He cupped the full softness of her white breast beneath its double covering. Her hardened nipple kissed his palm.

"My enchantress," he whispered, moving his head lower to kiss the tender area below her ear.

At once she saw herself as he did. Now the magic was hers, and she fancied herself as Morgan le Fay, casting a spell of love and desire. Suddenly he was a humble knight, all gold and silver, completely under her power. It was she who was willing him to continue giving her pleasure. Morgana moaned softly as his mouth moved lower, kissing her hot skin, murmuring of her beauty. His hand slid boldly lower beneath her skirts, then stroked upward along her firm thigh, leaving a trail of burning flesh.

Once more it was Nicholas who was magic. Without her knowing when it happened, he had sent Morgana to the heart of the void where a flame burned for them alone. It was dark red at first, the deep color of blood, of their hearts that now beat as one. Gradually it changed . . . heating to white-hot, blinding her . . . then to a bright silver, seducing her completely. The flame twisted, taking her with it. Morgana was lost, whirling in a void of fiery passion!

But somehow, another sound, one growing louder and more insistent, invaded Morgana's subconscious, forcing her to listen in spite of herself. The sound disturbed her so greatly that the spell was broken, taking with it the flame that had enveloped her only a minute before. She tried to ignore the sound and to recapture the feeling—impossible.

It was a voice—one familiar—and it was calling her name. Morgana's eyes flew open, extinguishing even the embers, and her fingers dug into Nicholas's shoulders as she realized it sounded like . . . Barney!

Understanding she had left their world of magic, finally hearing the voice, too, Nicholas reluctantly raised his head and moved so that Morgana could tighten the laces of her bodice and smooth her skirts.

Barney's tousled red head, topped with a green Robin Hood hat, appeared in the midst of the foliage. He burst into the clearing and seemed surprised at the scattered cups, scraps of food, and especially the flustered couple who stared at him with belligerent eyes.

"Hey, what are you two doing out here?" he asked as though nothing were wrong. "Having an orgy?"

The beginning of the return trip was dominated by Barney's cheerful banter. "I looked all over for you. Finally, someone told me you had trotted down the horse path."

Still embarrassed at having been caught in a compromising position, Morgana sat quietly, trying to sort through her muddled thoughts. She had teetered back and forth all day, thinking Nicholas was not her type, then admitting he had a definite attraction for her. Unfortunately she still could not forget that he didn't seem to take her profession seriously. And she had known him for only one week. How could she have warmed to him so easily? Perhaps "heated" was a more accurate term. If Barney hadn't interrupted when he had, anything might have happened!

She had no idea of Nicholas's thoughts. He also was subdued. Their new and untested relationship had too quickly reached a high level of intimacy, exposing her vulnerability.

Only when Nicholas slipped his hand over hers did she feel more at ease, finding comfort in its warmth.

Her enthusiasm reasserted itself, and she began to tell Barney about her ideas for the medieval wedding.

"We can have the bride and groom approach the wedding tent, riding down a treelined path—"

"On white palfreys!" boomed Barney.

"Yes. We'll have to check out the local stables. And I'll have to call the manager of the medieval restaurant you told me about. I hope they'll be willing to cater the reception."

"It'll be a first!" Barney began to gesture grandly as he steered the van down a ramp to the highway. "We must have the traditional mead, sweet honey cakes, a side of beef or two, a boar's—"

"No boar's head!" Morgana insisted vehemently.

"Boar's head?" Nicholas repeated.

"Oh, never mind. Don't pay any attention to him." Morgana gestured toward Barney. "He gets a little carried away with his authenticity sometimes."

He might not be interested, but Morgana wanted to include Nicholas in the conversation. She asked him, "What do you think of the ideas so far? Have any to add?"

"Actually I've seen and heard so much today that I'd like to sit back and digest it all for a while."

"Tired?" Morgana asked wonderingly.

"Oh, no," Nicholas assured her by squeezing her hand. "Actually I was thinking about how much I enjoyed myself today."

His vibrant tone made Morgana remember swirling colors and burning passion. Her pulse thudded erratically.

"Some kind of workday, huh?" Barney commented. "I don't know how people stand being cooped up in an office. It would drive me crazy!"

57

"Well, it's not as relaxing as spending a day in the open," Nicholas said in agreement.

"I guess it takes a more ordinary, uncomplicated personality to do that sort of work. Reams of white paper with little black figures are so uninspiring to the aesthetic soul."

"I'm sure," Nicholas said tersely.

Remembering Nicholas's earlier remarks about Barney, Morgana opened her mouth to change the conversation.

"I don't know how anyone can stand the blah-looking uniforms." Barney persevered. "Everything's black or gray or brown. After a while it must affect one's perception of life." Now Morgana was getting annoyed with Barney. She could feel Nicholas tense beside her. "Those high collars and ties would make me feel I was choking to death," Barney went on.

Imagining Barney dressed in suit and tie was too much for Morgana. She snorted. Then she and Barney burst into laughter.

"Gee, it must be nice to have such a *fun* occupation," Nicholas told them both sarcastically, emphasizing the word "fun." Obviously he wasn't going to take Barney's insults lying down.

"Fun! You've never had to sit up until four in the morning sewing a satin back crepe wedding dress!" Morgana protested.

"No, but then I don't get to do such unusual—*if enjoyable* —things with my clients either!"

Deftly she withdrew her hand. What did he mean by that? Did Nicholas think she entertained *all* her male clients with woodland picnics?

Nicholas didn't even try to recapture her hand. They both were silent for the remaining few miles. Even Barney seemed to be affected by the tension between them. Morgana couldn't wait to be alone with Nicholas. She had a few things to say to him once they were free of Barney's company.

Breathing a sigh of relief when they pulled up in front of her apartment, Morgana told Barney she'd see him in the morning. As the van moved out, Nicholas walked her to the door. She didn't try to stop him, but when he suggested he come in as though nothing were wrong, she turned on him.

"Entertaining clients in my apartment is not part of my *fun* occupation, Mr. Bedford," she insisted. "Nor is entertaining clients in the woods, I want you to know! This is the first time such a thing has happened, and I can *assure* you it will be the last!"

They were facing each other on the sidewalk. Morgana glared, her eyes hostile. Nicholas stood stiffly. His eyes glittered in return. "Really? Don't let me inhibit you."

Morgana couldn't resist voicing her angry disappointment. "I just knew you were one of those rigid business types. You're . . . a . . . a *banker.* You can't understand art, just money and power. I should have expected this."

Nicholas glared. "What are you talking about? What kind of preconceived notions do you have about my profession? Is that why you and your actor friend were trying to make fun of me?"

"We weren't making fun of you. We were amused by the situation!" she protested.

"What situation? The one in the woods? Did you have a fling in the woods with me to see how far an uptight banker type would go? Was I a challenge?" Before Morgana could answer, another thought struck him. "Did you arrange for Barney conveniently to interrupt us so you wouldn't get too involved?"

"I can't believe this!" Morgana sputtered. "I don't want

to continue this conversation. We are obviously from separate worlds. You can go back to your reams of paper, and I'll return to my frivolity! I'm sure we can work out the details of your sister's wedding with a minimum of contact. You aren't interested in it anyway."

Nicholas stood frozen as Morgana pushed by him, flouncing toward her door. "Rather high-handed of you to decide that for me," he growled. "But then you seem to be good at making assumptions."

"Where are my keys?" she muttered, frustrated when she couldn't find them. She couldn't even make a dramatic exit!

"We've got more important things to settle than finding your damn keys!" Nicholas insisted.

"You may not think my business is important, Mr. Bedford, but I have a lot of work to do tomorrow!" she shouted, dumping the entire contents of her purse on the ground in frustration. "I'm going to get some sleep!"

"Fine!" Nicholas retorted. Then he stalked away and almost jumped into his car.

Watching him drive away, Morgana realized there was metal digging into her left palm. Relaxing her fist, she stared at the elusive keys. She'd been holding them all along. Groaning, she knelt to pick up the scattered objects from her sidewalk.

Their tryst in the forest seemed to have happened in another century.

CHAPTER FOUR

"Beautiful!" said Morgana as she entered the Manor, the restaurant chosen for the Victorian wedding reception. Standing on an Oriental rug that covered the polished wooden floor of the entrance hallway, she looked around her. Above her head hung an elaborate crystal chandelier. A champagne fountain had been erected in the curtained alcove near the restaurant's front door. She watched the cascade of golden, bubbling liquid and inhaled the ripe smell of orange blossoms. The florist had cleverly entwined the delicate flowers around the banisters of the staircase leading to the second floor of the renovated Victorian mansion.

A perfect setting for a perfectly executed wedding. Morgana was pleased with her arrangements for the Matthews marriage. Now she had only to make a last-minute inspection of the Manor's premises before the arrival of the bridal party. She would have sufficient time. The bride, groom, and attendants were being transported from the church by horse and carriage. They were bound to make slow progress, even on a Sunday evening in the suburbs.

She poked her head into the "library," one of the dining rooms on the mansion's first floor. Clusters of immaculate linen-topped tables met her eye, each crowned with an arrangement of orange blossoms surrounding glass-enclosed candles. Beyond the tables stood the massively carved wooden bar area.

"Excuse me."

She moved aside for a black-suited waiter brandishing a long matchstick. Methodically he began to light the tables' candles. Flickering candlelight would pick up the richness of the Manor's interior: the velvet-upholstered spoon-backed chairs, flocked wallpaper, stained glass, and mirrors.

At the sound of a door opening, Morgana turned. Two early guests were greeted by the maître d'. He then saw Morgana.

"Good evening, Miss Lawrence. Everything's going fine. Have you seen the gold room?" He opened a door on the opposite side of the hallway, revealing the room's moiré-lined interior. Tables had been pushed together for the purpose of displaying wedding gifts. Stacks of colorfully wrapped items were already in evidence.

"The place looks lovely," Morgana said assuringly.

"And so do you, Miss Lawrence, if I may say so."

"Thank you."

She *did* look lovely, she conceded, mounting the mahogany staircase. As if to second her opinion, she came face-to-face with her reflection in a long beveled mirror on the first landing. She sparkled back at herself, the pink roses pinned into her dark hair adding a subtle color to her complexion. Pulling up her long skirts, she ascended the second flight of steps. She was happy she had taken the time to make a period piece dress for herself. The rose-colored polished cotton dress, with its low sweetheart neckline and cap sleeves, could be worn in most seasons. The bustlelike gathering of fabric at the hips made the gown appropriate for any future Victorian weddings she was sure to design. *I'm in bloom,* she thought, looking down at the rose color.

The phrase stuck in her mind as she entered the upstairs banquet room. "Blooming" was a word usually reserved for women in love. Or at least involved with a man. Unbidden, her memories of Nicholas Bedford surfaced. His hands, his lips, his eyes. Caresses in a forest glade. A last, painfully angry encounter. Morgana shook herself. She had refused to think about Nicholas for days, and she wasn't going to start again now. She had more important things to do.

A quickly appraising glance showed her that the upstairs tables were as beautifully set as those in the library. She was alone in the large room with a waiter obviously in charge of setting up the buffet table.

"Some feast, huh?" The dark young man eyed Morgana. "You're a little early. There'll be a round of beef and several more hot dishes. We're in the process of putting them out."

Morgana surveyed the long table, complete with central flower arrangement and silver candlesticks.

"I'm Morgana Lawrence. From Fantasy Weddings."

"Oh. You're checking things out. Like what you see?"

The delicate odor of salmon en croûte teased Morgana's nostrils. There were glass bowls of whole shrimp, salad, fresh fruit, and croissants, as well as hot dishes on warmers. She was pleased to note a couple of elaborately molded aspics, complete with ribbons and leaves trimming their tops.

"Those look very Victorian." Morgana smiled with satisfaction.

"There's going to be a trifle with the desserts, too," the waiter told her. "Sponge cake soaked in rum and liquor topped with a custard sauce. It'll be placed down there." He indicated the far end of the table. "Close to the wedding cake."

"The Manor's done a very nice job."

"Well, we hope you'll be doing more events here."

Smiling, Morgana congratulated herself on the Matthews wedding. Times like this made her long work hours worthwhile and her problems with Blanche of secondary importance. She mustn't forget she now had her own business and no longer had to deal with Miles's controlling stranglehold, which limited her talents. That all was behind her now.

Moving around the buffet table, Morgana was aware of distant murmuring accompanying the arrival of more guests in the downstairs hallway.

"The bride is coming! The bride is coming!"

She heard the shouts from below. Descending the stairs to the landing, Morgana looked down. The new Mrs. Lawrence Matthews burst through the door of the Manor, her cheeks flushed with excitement, her brown curls disarrayed beneath a circlet of orange blossoms and veil. Guests flowed by and around the nuptial pair, who smiled for the flash of a camera. The bride preened, smoothing her hair for yet another picture. The white satin of her two-piece wedding dress gleamed luxuriously in the chandelier's light. The garment had been designed with a small bustle and train. Its square décolletage, cap sleeves, and hem edges were trimmed with cream-colored ribbon and lace.

An authentic 1870s Victorian touch, Morgana thought with satisfaction; two fabrics of similar colors were often combined during that period. She had also fashioned the three bridesmaids' dresses in varying shades of pastels. Morgana took one last look. The groom stood with his arm around the bride, his black swallowtail coat emphasizing the whiteness of his waistcoat, formal shirt, and cravat.

"Morgana!"

She saw Mrs. Templeton, the bride's mother, approaching. The stout woman was puffing a little as she climbed the stairway in her long blue lace dress.

"Morgana, it was just beautiful!" Mrs. Templeton had reached the landing and touched Morgana's arm. "You made such a fabulous dress for my baby. And this wedding will be remembered forever."

Mrs. Templeton moved on to converse with another guest. They were headed for the buffet room. People had been filing up the stairway in the short time Morgana was standing there, among them the musicians. She could hear the group warming up in the room above.

She quickly decided she should have something to eat. Much of the remaining evening would be spent talking to friends and acquaintances of the bridal pair, making contacts. In the absence of Blanche, Morgana was Fantasy Weddings' only representative.

She was about to help herself to the salmon or crepes when Morgana felt an odd, prickling sensation at the nape of her neck. Someone was watching. She turned from the buffet table and froze.

Nicholas Bedford stood framed in the doorway of the banquet room. Shimmering candlelight picked up the silver in his embroidered waistcoat. The garment fitted him well, outlining his trim physique beneath a black tuxedo jacket. He didn't smile or nod. He stared.

Morgana's throat constricted. She couldn't tear her eyes away, yet she dreaded another ugly confrontation. In her determination to put Nicholas out of her mind, she had forgotten that he would certainly be a wedding guest of his friend Larry Matthews.

Continuing eye contact, Nicholas walked coolly across the room. His demeanor was serious, and she was surprised by his opening remark. "You seem to have done a fine job with this wedding, Morgana. I'm quite impressed."

She didn't respond.

"I'm sure you'll do as well with Mari's wedding. I'm looking forward to it."

"I intend to do a *fantastic* job." Morgana kept the quiver out of her voice. Here she was, getting defensive again. Nicholas's presence was like an electric shock.

"Would you like to dance?"

"Dance?"

Morgana had been standing near the room's long central table, about to pick up a plate. She hadn't noticed the couples on the dance floor, moving to the quartet's waltzlike strains.

"I don't feel like dancing at the moment."

"Oh, come on. I know you like it. I've seen you cavorting on the forest paths, remember."

Placing a hand on the small of her back, Nicholas firmly swung a surprised and unresisting Morgana onto the dancing area, then into his arms. Looking up, Morgana saw they were almost nose to nose.

"I think we should talk about a reconciliation. Peace," stated Nicholas. They stepped gently to the waltz's rhythm. Morgana's body responded unconsciously, moving gracefully against Nicholas, her hand warmed by his grasp. It would be natural to melt into his arms.

"I think we both should apologize," Nicholas continued intently.

"Me? Apologize?" Morgana felt her anger begin to rise. "You were the one who made serious accusations. An apology is not enough."

"How about six or seven apologies then?"

"I don't find that humorous."

They were circling the small dance floor when the quartet's sounds changed, blending into a contemporary tune. Nicholas pulled Morgana closer. Changing rhythm and di-

66

rection, his knees brushed her inner thighs, making them tingle.

"Look," he explained, "I was irritated and tired. I think I misinterpreted a few things. Then you lost your temper."

Morgana confronted him. "I had good reason to be angry!"

"Yes. I admit I was way out of line, and I apologize. I don't know what got into me." His tone was sincere. "Please give us the chance . . . to get to know each other better."

In spite of her attempt to frown, Morgana's face softened, her lips curving into a smile. She wanted to forgive him.

"I love it when you look like that." Nicholas's breath fanned her face. "I'd like to know more ways to make you smile. I already know enough ways to make you angry." His searching gaze warmed her.

Then, as if to ease the rising erotic tension between them, Morgana pulled away slightly. "All right. I'm willing to start over. You may have been receiving negative vibrations from me. When I first saw you, I thought you resembled the banker I had to deal with—beg, actually—to get a loan to start my half of Fantasy Weddings. Your three-piece suit reminded me of Blanche's uptight husband. He's a lawyer who thoroughly disapproves of me."

"Well, I completely approve."

She wondered if he meant her business or herself. Nicholas drew Morgana closer again, his smoothly shaved jaw rubbing against her temple.

"We take a lot of things too seriously." His voice was gentle above her ear. "I mean, Fantasy Weddings isn't going to change the world. It's not like nuclear armament or the world money market. But I guess your job is as good as any until something better comes along."

Slowly Morgana stiffened. The man was insulting her

again. How condescending! He softened her up with a little apology, then revealed what he really thought. Her reply was tart. "Well, in view of the state of the world, a little added creativity could be infinitely useful."

Nicholas glanced down at her, surprised.

"I want to sit down." She was calm, simply staring coldly at him.

"Uh-oh. I see we're going to have to start all over again."

Morgana tried to pull away, but Nicholas tightened his grip. "No, you don't. Not this time." She felt entrapped.

"I *said* I want to sit down," Morgana hissed.

"And I said I think we can work this out."

If Morgana struggled to get away, it was sure to cause a scene. She looked around. All right, if the man wanted to dance, they'd dance!

Taking the lead, she suddenly executed a complicated step, causing Nicholas to stumble. He caught himself and pulled her even closer. Their bodies touched. The combination of erotic tension and her anger was raising Morgana's adrenaline to unprecedented heights. Firmly she pushed against Nicholas's hand. His greater strength neutralized her action. She stepped in the opposite direction of his rhythm and accidentally stamped his foot. Nicholas responded by unexpectedly whirling her in a circle and back into his arms. Morgana almost lost an evening sandal. They were locked in a close embrace, breathing heavily and glaring at each other.

He murmured, "You're impossible."

Morgana was receiving unexpected pleasure with the release of her aggressions. She deliberately continued to push and pull at Nicholas, who stubbornly held on.

Perhaps it was the quiet tittering that finally alerted the engrossed couple. Both suddenly realized that the music had stopped. But when had it stopped? How long had they been publicly struggling on the dance floor without music, to the guests' amusement?

Morgana proudly walked to a nearby table, her features infused with color. She was happy to see that Nicholas's classic cheekbones seemed to be turning pink. They sat down, Nicholas politely pulling out her chair.

Morgana struggled to retain her composure. Was Nicholas going to grin? The corners of his mouth twitched, and tiny wrinkles were forming about his eyes. Morgana covered her mouth with her hand, but their laughter was inevitable. It bubbled forth like a froth of champagne. Nicholas snorted. Morgana's shoulders shook. Soon they both were laughing so hard that there were tears in their eyes.

Morgana thought she heard Mrs. Templeton talking earnestly nearby. "Isn't it nice? They're having *such* a good time."

Nicholas removed an impeccable white silk handkerchief from his breast pocket and wiped his eyes. He offered it to Morgana. "You've got to admit we have one thing in common. We've both got a sense of humor."

"Or a sense of the ridiculous," she gasped, attempting to catch her breath.

Nicholas jokingly held up his hands. "Okay. Peace? Truce? Forgive me?"

Morgana sobered. "Please get this straight. I take my profession seriously. I'm not running my wedding business until 'something better' comes along. I intend to make Fantasy Weddings succeed if I have to do it by myself. It's very important to me—"

Nicholas interrupted. "I wasn't trying to demean it. I seem to keep putting my foot in my mouth." He leaned toward her, intent in his sincerity. "I have a sarcastic view of work in general, my own included. *I* don't like to work long hours. Maybe I'm a little envious of creative people like you, so passionately devoted to what they do. Reams of figures may bore me more than I realized." He raised his eyebrows. "I find *your* figure much more interesting."

Morgana tried to keep a straight face. Why did he have to be so witty?

The uncomfortable strain between them had disappeared for the moment. Their laughter had produced a new sense of camaraderie. Morgana felt warmed by the stimulating connection. She also felt hungry.

"Let's get something to eat."

"Shall I get you a plate?" he asked.

Morgana thought for a second. "No. I want to look at the food. I couldn't make up my mind before. I'd been drooling over that buffet for at least an hour."

Nicholas left his jacket to save their chairs. Numerous wedding guests were milling around. The room was almost full.

They helped themselves to assorted delicacies and returned to their table. She was grateful to see they still had it to themselves. Not that it mattered. When she was in the presence of the silver-eyed hypnotist, all other people seemed to recede around her.

The strains of classical music in the background enhanced Morgana's mood. She admired Nicholas's sharply etched profile. He could look so severe, but when he relaxed, he was handsome. The silver-embroidered waistcoat was a nice touch. She could imagine him as a Victorian gentleman. And she would be a Victorian lady, she thought, continuing the fantasy. No, Morgana decided, she didn't want to be that kind of lady. She would be an artistic type, like Sarah

Bernhardt, and she and Nicholas were having dinner in a London club . . .

"What are you thinking about?" Nicholas asked. "You seem to be a million miles away."

Morgana became aware of her surroundings. Nicholas's knee brushed against her own beneath the tablecloth, causing sensations to shiver up her leg. "I was just dreaming, fantasizing. It's a way I have of using my imagination."

"I hope they were good."

Horrified, Morgana thought he was going to ask her for specifics. "My fantasies?"

"No. The shrimp."

"Huh? I don't know."

"You just ate six. Now you have sauce on your face." Before she could react, Nicholas picked up his napkin and carefully wiped her chin. "I wouldn't want sauce to mar your delicate beauty."

Morgana sighed with relief. Someday her imagination was going to get her into trouble.

"Morgana!" Sharon Templeton Matthews interrupted. "I've been looking all over for you." The bride had shed her crown of orange blossoms, but her young face glowed in the candlelight. "Some friends want to meet you. They might be interested in one of your weddings. Oh, am I interrupting?"

Morgana hesitated.

"It's all right. I know you have your job to do." Nicholas seemed to reassure her.

"Okay. I'd like to meet them," she told Sharon, then to Nicholas: "I'll be back."

"They" turned out to be six different people. Morgana talked to all, although she knew she'd be lucky if one of them contacted her in the future. Once during the lengthy discussions she turned and saw Nicholas still sitting at their

71

table. Later she noticed him standing near the banquet room door. He was motioning and mouthing something. *He must be going downstairs,* she thought, returning her attention to the woman at her side. Handing the prospective client one of her terra-cotta and blue business cards, Morgana suggested the woman call the Fantasy Weddings office, then went in search of Nicholas.

He wasn't downstairs. She looked in every room, even waited outside the men's rest room for a few minutes. After receiving a particularly curious stare, she gave up and looked out the front door. Obviously Nicholas had gone. He must have been trying to tell her he had to leave.

She felt a sense of loss, of disappointment. When would she see him next? Where had he gone? Startled, Morgana recognized her dawning feelings. It had been not only Nicholas's businesslike appearance that had put her off but, more deeply, his magnetic appeal for her. He signified a possible romantic relationship—one she didn't want.

Careful, she thought, admonishing herself. Miles had been handsome and charming, too. After her devastating experience with him, ending only a year ago, was she ready for another man? Morgana determined to proceed with caution.

CHAPTER FIVE

Morgana's attention kept wandering as she tried to finish the alterations on Mariette's wedding dress. No wonder. It was late Saturday afternoon. The medieval costume fittings had been that morning, and she'd been busy ever since. Her part-time seamstress, Carla, had already left for home after altering clothing for the groom, best man, and maid of honor.

Morgana slowed as she thought about fitting Nicholas for his costume. Her lips curved into a happy smile as she remembered his discomfort while her hands moved over his body, tucking and pinning. She'd taken full advantage of him, and he'd known it! His eyes had glittered dangerously, and before changing into his street clothes, he had whispered something about getting revenge. Morgana was impatient to see what form it took!

Since the Victorian wedding his attitude had been one of friendly flirtatiousness. It wasn't every day Morgana met a man who could stir her most secret feelings. There was a magic about Nicholas she couldn't resist, even when she tried to slow it down.

Perhaps it was better this way. Morgana forced herself back to the task at hand. Nicholas seemed determined to limit overinvolvement for both of them. Morgana sighed.

Having finished Mari's dress, she was hanging it up when Barney sauntered in.

"Morgana, darling! The gown is truly stunning!" he declared, striking a theatrical pose.

Morgana bit her lip as she glanced up. Should she comment on the helmet he was wearing? He'd be disappointed if she didn't.

"Great headgear, Barney. What, no chain mail?"

"Well, I didn't want to overdo." Barney removed the purple and yellow plumed headpiece and sighed. "So where is he?"

"Who?"

"Lover boy. Bedford has been here so often I was starting to think of him as one of the fixtures!"

"Barney, you *are* exaggerating. Nicholas has been here to make approvals."

Actually not only had Nicholas made approvals, but he had come up with a terrific idea of his own: A troubadour would guide the guests through the ceremony, explaining the origins of certain wedding customs in specially written prose. He would also recite romantic poems and serenade the guests with love ballads.

"He seems devoted to you, Morgana," Barney teased. "I assume the feeling is mutual?"

Morgana reddened. She'd acted casual about Nicholas, but Barney could see through her. She grabbed Nicholas's costume and sat back down at a sewing machine.

"Did you stop by to give me a hard time, Barney?" she asked.

"Don't get too excited, Morgana, darling, but I've found a first-rate substitute for the boar's head!"

"No boar's head!" they bellowed in unison, then burst into laughter.

"Picture this," Barney began dramatically, using his hands to frame their imaginary view. "A procession of appropriately garbed lads and wenches carrying trays laden with food for the buffet. At the head is a magnificent white swan, the symbol of fidelity. Imagine the stunned reaction of the guests as they note the proud arched neck, the pure white plumage, a tiny gold crown on its head."

"You want me to put a live swan on the buffet table?"

"Not live. Cooked, feathers intact. They did that for medieval feasts, you know. Special occasions only, of course."

Morgana's stomach churned. Fighting the queasiness, she sighed. "Barney, whatever will you come up with next?"

"Actually a swan *would* add a nice touch." A familiar voice intruded.

"Nicholas!" Startled, Morgana wondered what he was doing there. Two appearances in one day? Her heart thudded unevenly as she wondered if he'd come to seek the revenge he'd threatened.

"Cooking a swan, feathers and all, might be a bit much, though. What about a swan-shaped cake?" Nicholas suggested.

"Capital idea!" Barney agreed. "All the drama without the gore." With that, Barney headed for the door. "Mission accomplished!"

"Try to be on time Monday, will you?" Morgana called after him. Facing Nicholas, she felt elated yet nervous.

"So what about you?" Nicholas asked, staring at her intently. "Do you think it's a capital idea?"

"Yes. I also think you're a stabilizing influence on Barney."

"He does have a flair for the dramatic, doesn't he? I haven't seen him around much the last week," Nicholas commented from the other side of her sewing machine.

75

"He's been in and out, running errands. Punctuality is not one of his strong points, but for the most part Barney is worth his weight in gold. He's terribly creative." How long would Nicholas stand over her like that?

"I thought I'd stop by to see if there was anything I could do for you."

Morgana was sorely tempted to give him a list! But far be it from her to carry the conversation to that personal a level. Blood pounded in her ears as she raised her eyes to meet his.

"Are you good with a needle and thread?" she asked.

"Actually it's not one of my fortes. However, I wouldn't mind trying on my costume for you again if you promised to check the fit as carefully as you did the last time."

He was leaning over the sewing machine toward her, stroking the material. Their fingers touched, and she felt burned. Could this be his revenge, to tease her and then do nothing about it? Morgana had a nasty inspiration.

"The checks and invoices!" She would put him to work, all right! Heading for the office, Morgana said, "I hate to trouble you, but if you're serious, you could enter the checks into the journal, then put them in their envelopes with their appropriate invoices. Not a very exciting task, I'm afraid."

"I think I can handle it," Nicholas said assuringly. "Blanche didn't show up today, huh?" he asked as he made himself comfortable behind her desk.

"No. She must have found something more important to do," Morgana said, excusing her sister.

Nicholas was not so easily fooled. "Like getting her hair done?"

Morgana's eyes widened slightly. He must have overheard their conversation the first day he came to the shop with Mari. And Blanche had been so certain their new clients hadn't heard a thing!

76

"You know, as many times as I've been here this week, I haven't seen Blanche around once," Nicholas continued.

"That's Blanche, a regular will-o'-the-wisp," Morgana said with a chuckle.

"Must be hard, running a business all by yourself. No wonder you work twelve hours a day!" Nicholas growled.

"I'm used to it." Morgana shrugged off his concern, but she was flattered. "Now make sure the right invoices get in the right envelopes, would you?"

Nicholas immediately got to work making the entries. He didn't spare her another glance, but Morgana was sure his lips twitched in amusement as she backed out the door.

Morgana hated to leave her office. Reluctantly she returned to her own work, but within minutes she was busy and humming contentedly. Rather than distract her, Nicholas seemed to inspire her to work. It was odd, knowing he was in the next room, working, too. But somehow, it was comforting.

The fact that Nicholas showed up a second time in one day *and* offered to help when there was no reason—none connected with his sister's wedding, that is—was proof enough for Morgana that he was definitely interested in her. As for his subtle plan for revenge, Morgana would find a way to foil it!

Awhile later—it seemed like minutes, although Morgana knew it was closer to an hour—she felt Nicholas watching her.

"Hi there. All done?"

"Every invoice and check in the right envelope," he said, not moving from the doorway. He leaned against the framework in an indolent and sexy manner. "I'm impressed. From what I could gather from your books, you've got a thriving business here."

"Could be better with more clients."

"Advertise."

"The truth is, I couldn't handle additional weddings. I'm overloaded with work as it is."

"Maybe if you had a partner who really did half the work, you could."

"I'd like that," she said wistfully. "All I want to do is design the garments and oversee the creative aspects of the business. Oh, well, maybe someday." She really didn't want to talk about Blanche any more than she had wanted to talk about Barney. Morgana was becoming annoyed. Was Nicholas thickheaded or what? Peevishly she turned her attention back to the wedding dress.

"You know what time it is?"

"I'm afraid not," Morgana answered over the whine of the sewing machine.

"It's time to get something to eat. How about my place?"

"What?" Morgana almost sewed her fingers to the garment. She stopped the machine and turned her rapt attention to him.

"I'm not a very good cook, but I do know how to grill steaks and toss a salad. How about it?"

How about it? Morgana felt like cheering. Instead, she managed a cool "Sure. Sounds good. A woman's got to eat." But she couldn't keep the sparkle of happiness from her eyes.

"Can you be at my place in an hour?"

Nicholas gave her directions to his town house complex, then left. Morgana danced her way up the stairs, giggling with glee. She'd dazzle Nicholas tonight. Plans for revenge or no, he'd have to be dead to resist her!

An hour later Morgana was driving up the winding road to his town house. The guard at the complex gate had called Nicholas, warning him of her arrival. She found his place easily, for Nicholas was standing in the doorway waiting for her.

Morgana was startled by his appearance. Well-worn, low-slung jeans molded his lightly muscular thighs. A thin gauze shirt barely covered his chest. Through it, she could see his nipples and a soft mat of silver-brown hair. She wasn't prepared for his unexpected informality, but she liked it. Even his feet were bare.

"Right on time," Nicholas said as he helped her out of the car. His low whistle of appreciation bolstered Morgana's confidence.

"Thanks. I'm glad you approve."

Morgana wore a hand-painted silk wrap dress that left one shoulder bare. Set on a background of deepest turquoise, shooting stars and slivers of moons were interspersed along the outside edge of her wrap.

"You wore my necklace." His voice held warm approval.

"It's perfect with this dress, don't you think?"

"That's not all that's perfect," he murmured as they entered his home. As she walked, Morgana knew her dress alternately clung to, then flared out from her legs. She made the most of the provocative display, swaying her slender hips with deliberation. Her reward was the gratifying sound of Nicholas sucking in his breath.

The entryway led into a huge living area with dining nook. A good-sized kitchen was off to the left.

"Very elegant," Morgana said, complimenting him. Pale gray walls and carpeting set off the charcoal gray sectional sofa that snaked around one corner of the room. The coffee and dining tables were of black glass, and the half dozen dining chairs were upholstered in the same dark gray as the couch.

"It's comfortable," Nicholas told her. There was a pride in his voice that make Morgana wonder if he'd decorated it himself.

She eyed a recessed area, mirrored with black glass shelves. Track lighting accented a small collection of artifacts—Egyptian, Roman, Peruvian. The pieces looked as valuable as the colorful modern paintings gracing the walls. Comfortable indeed!

"Let's go outside. I'll throw the steaks on the grill."

Morgana followed him out the sliding glass doors onto the wood deck. Latticework surrounding it served as trellises for flowering vines. The grill was built-in, as was the semicircular seating area covered with plushy patterned cushions. The view was spectacular: a man-made lake framed by weeping willow trees.

"Could you get the salad from the fridge? And the plates and flatware are on the counter."

"Be right back."

Morgana kicked off her high-heeled sandals once she was inside the sliding glass doors. She loved the plush feeling of the rug beneath her naked toes. She was in the black and white tiled kitchen only a few minutes before reappearing on the deck with her arms full.

"M-m-m. Smells delicious," she told Nicholas, leaning over the grill, giving him a perfect view of the top of her breasts. In the midst of turning the steaks, he almost dropped one into the coals.

Smiling with satisfaction, Morgana set the table.

"Do you think forks are necessary?" Nicholas asked. "We could eat medieval style. With our fingers."

In a low, sexy voice Morgana replied, "Surely we can think of better things to do with our hands."

For a second she thought he might not take the bait. Then he growled, "You'd better be careful or you might find out what knights do to their errant ladies."

His gray eyes contained banked fires, and Morgana was hard pressed not to say, "Show me." She made herself comfortable while he crossed to the cart and opened the wine. When he handed her a glass of ruby wine, he couldn't miss the length of her bare leg since she'd opened the wrap to mid-thigh.

"The steaks are ready if you like yours rare."

"The juicier, the better," she said in a sexy voice.

Nicholas blinked hard and shook his head. He speared the steaks, then added them, foil-wrapped baked potatoes, and warmed rolls to the plates. "Not fancy, but filling."

He slid next to Morgana but left too much room between them for her liking. She inched closer to him and inhaled the pleasing mixture of aftershave and grilled steak. The scent awakened more than one appetite.

Nicholas ate with his fingers. After reaching past him, allowing her breast to brush against his arm, Morgana snatched a piece of meat from his plate and popped it into her mouth. Nicholas stared.

Silver flecks leaped from his eyes as he challenged her. "Aren't you going to feed me, too? The way you did at the fair?"

Excitement fluttered through Morgana. Her breathing grew shallow; her movement, leisurely. Having taken a piece of meat from her own plate, she held it inches from his mouth. Nicholas dipped his head to capture her fingers along with the juicy beef. Her toes curled when he began to suck on her fingertips.

81

When he raised his head from that erotic task, his face was scant inches from hers. "M-m-m, nice." He breathed softly.

Morgana couldn't help herself. She closed the small gap between them and touched her mouth to his. She meant it to be only a whisper of a kiss. A tease. A promise of delight. But somehow, her bare foot found his and slid up under his jeans leg along his warm skin. The contact was electrifying, making her bolder. After slipping her hand inside his shirt, Morgana felt the strong beat of his heart and the warmth of his flesh.

The kiss deepened, and Morgana touched her tongue to his. Nicholas wasn't resisting her, but neither was he taking command of the situation as she thought he would. The frustration of the last week finally got to her. The least he could do was kiss her properly! Morgana nipped his lower lip as if to get his attention, then kissed him once more with feeling.

Why couldn't he kiss her as he had at the Faire? Where was the modern-day magician who had cast her under his spell and then called her his enchantress? As her soft lips and eager tongue assaulted his mouth—as Morgana willed Nicholas to respond—the feelings they shared that day came back to haunt her. Morgana lost herself in that kiss, and suddenly Nicholas came alive. Her heart soared as he transformed her from seductress to the seduced.

His eyes were open, as were hers. He used them to spin a silver web around her. There was no escape even if she sought one, for Nicholas was transformed into her sorcerer with the power to hypnotize, to tantalize. Morgana hadn't meant to push him this far. A kiss—that's all she had desired for the moment. His eyes promised—no, demanded—more.

His hot hands found the sweet spots along her spine. Through the silken material they stroked her back, leaving a trail of gooseflesh that chilled her. Morgana pressed closer to Nicholas to absorb his warmth. Her fingers stroked his chest, moving deeper under the gauze shirt. When a fingertip lightly skimmed over a nipple, it hardened. Nicholas sucked in his breath.

"That's it!" he growled, standing and pulling her with him.

"Nicholas?" It was a question and a plea. Why was he interrupting their delightful embrace? Morgana couldn't have been more surprised when he drew her toward him, away from the table.

"Just remember, you started this!" he said warningly.

"But what about the food?" she asked weakly. As if she cared!

"You've roused other appetites in me, milady," Nicholas answered wickedly. Before she knew what was happening, Morgana found herself balanced over his shoulder and on the way to the sliding glass doors.

"Nicholas!" she protested, not knowing what to make of his behavior. Then they were through the doors and in his living room. "Nicholas, what are you doing?"

Within seconds Morgana found herself unceremoniously dumped on the carpeting. Before she had time to blink, Nicholas was on top of her. "I told you to beware lest you find out what knights do to their errant ladies," he growled before attacking her mouth.

Her lips felt bruised and battered under his onslaught, but Morgana yielded under his assault.

His kiss gentled, and Nicholas allowed his fingers to stroke her throat. His hand was restless, not content to stay in that one sweet place for long. It followed the line of her

83

shoulder, then dropped to her breast. The feel of the thin material against her nipple excited Morgana beyond belief, yet when he tried to pull the silk away, she cried out, "My dress."

"What?" His arched eyebrow made her feel foolish at the protest.

"If you only knew how many dozens of hours it took to hand-paint this, you'd—"

Before she could finish her weak complaint, Nicholas rolled to one side, freeing her. "Well, then, take it off."

"What?" she asked.

"Methinks milady is becoming hard-of-hearing," he said teasingly. On his side, Nicholas rested his head on one arm and stared at her. He trailed the fingers of his free hand up her arm and over her bare shoulder. Gentle fingertips found her breast and dipped inside the silken covering. Her hardened nipple pouted at him through the material, catching his complete interest. He asked softly, "So why don't you take this off and seduce me properly?"

Morgana hesitated. This had started as a game. She had been determined to make Nicholas demonstrate his interest in her. Nothing more. She had wanted their relationship to go beyond their choosing foods for Mari's wedding together. When exactly had she lost control?

But, then, what had she expected? She had deliberately provoked Nicholas so that he would stop treating her with that casual friendliness he had affected all week. The results had far exceeded her expectations. Did she want to commit herself so totally? She could be hurt again.

Morgana stared into Nicholas's silver-flecked eyes and was lost. Nicholas wasn't Miles. Always truthful with herself, Morgana had to admit she wanted to do exactly as Nicholas suggested. She would take the risk.

Her eyes never left his as her hands found the hooks and snaps that kept her wrap dress together. Languorously peeling it from her body, Morgana flushed. He was studying her intently. Would he be pleased? Although the sun was sinking across the lake, there was still enough light in the room to uncover every imperfection. His eyes glittered as she bared herself to him, and if Nicholas found fault, he gave no sign.

She thought he might touch her as she leaned over his body to place the dress on the couch. He didn't. With only a scrap of lace hiding her from him, Morgana sat back, not sure of what to do next. She was amazed that she felt not a bit of embarrassment with Nicholas. Perhaps it was because what they were doing was so right.

"Now you can undress *me*," he gently commanded. The silver-hot fires in his eyes willed Morgana to do as he directed. Nicholas rolled onto his back, stretched his arms straight out from his sides, and said dramatically, "Do with me what thou wilt, fair lady."

His teasing banter relaxed Morgana completely and sparked her imagination. As she mounted his thighs, Morgana saw not a simple shirt but an undertunic designed to protect her lord's skin from the abuse of his armor. Slipping her hands under it, she pushed the garment up toward his head. She took the opportunity to stroke his chest so she could feel the silken hair that had teased her through the gauze. Nicholas's stomach went taut, and he caught his breath at the bold touch of her fingers.

"Are my hands too cold, milord?" she asked teasingly. "I can avoid touching you if that is your pleasure."

"No, not cold" was all he could mutter.

"Then you don't wish me to stop?"

"No!"

Morgana chuckled at the anxiety she saw written on his face. It was obvious that Nicholas didn't care for her laughter, for he wrapped a hand around the back of her neck and pulled her to him, smothering the sound with his lips. Her breasts were crushed against his chest as he ground his mouth against hers.

All thoughts of play vanished as Nicholas summoned their magic with his lips. If Morgana had any doubts about sharing herself with Nicholas, he made them all vanish. He roused in her feelings that went beyond physical passion. Her heart and her head were involved as well. Morgana didn't know how to give herself any other way.

When Nicholas allowed her to breathe, releasing her lips so that he could kiss her chin, her neck, her shoulder, Morgana used a hand against his chest to push herself away.

Determined to finish the job she had started, she pulled the gauze shirt over his arms and then his head. Nicholas watched her as she next attacked his jeans. Straddling his thighs, Morgana unsnapped, then unzipped them. It was then she made a startling discovery. He wasn't wearing any underwear! Morgana gulped as she encountered the result of her lighthearted seduction. She was stunned by the enormousness of her success.

She was still staring when she felt Nicholas's hands on her. Starting at the outside of her thighs, they made small, intimate circles toward her lace-covered center. One of his hands remained there to tantalize her through the cloth as the other crept up her stomach, stopping only when it found a breast to fondle. Morgana was stunned by the force of her own response. She moaned, not able to suppress the sound of her need. Her eyes closed, and her body swayed closer to his so that it pressed heavily into his hands.

Nicholas groaned in response and pulled her to him, sliding her up slightly so that their bodies touched at perfect points. He held Morgana's face in his hands as he pressed into her. Morgana was anxious to rid herself of the lace barrier that prevented her from more intimate contact, but for the moment she hadn't the power to make her body function. She was lost in a world of sensation, one that Nicholas was creating for her with his hands, his lips, his hot skin sliding against her own.

Time receded. Morgana felt Nicholas reach out to take her, and it was as if a tornado were spinning her to its white-hot center. She let herself float.

Opening her eyes, she realized Nicholas was now over her, divesting himself of his jeans as his mouth made a moist trail from her face to her breasts. There he was not content with mere kisses. His tongue encouraged her nipples into hard, tight buds; he sucked them gently as if to draw out their sweetness. At the same time he rid her of their last barrier, then rediscovered her center of sensation. Morgana arched into his hand, wanting more than the teasing touch of his fingers.

"Nicholas, please," she whispered as the room began to spin. Her hands gripped his upper arms, trying to pull him over her.

Nicholas ignored her plea. Although he rubbed himself against her, continuing his assault through lips, teeth, and hands, he made no other move. Morgana was becoming frantic as a delightful pressure built within her. When she closed her eyes, she could see colors beckoning to her. Red, white, silver. Flames threatened to consume her. Morgana closed her eyes tighter so she could see them more clearly, then lost herself to their lure. It wouldn't be much longer before she was lost completely. . . .

"Nicholas, now . . . you must . . ." she pleaded, pushing at him with her body, trying to pull him into her by sheer will.

Then she was able to protest no more as her body arched even higher. The colors began to whirl. A long, low moan of pleasure started deep in her throat. It was at that point she sensed something had changed. Nicholas had moved. She opened her eyes to look into his silver ones poised over her. As he plunged into her, her lids dropped once more. A moan burst through her lips. Her body was suspended for a few agonizing seconds before it exploded with sensation.

A fine film of sweat covered her body when the sensation settled into little tremors. A frown creased her brow. Nicholas hadn't joined her. She could feel the proof of his unrelieved passion deep inside her.

"Why?" she asked, gazing into his eyes. She stroked his silver-streaked hair and felt a shudder run through him. "Why did you wait so long?"

His smile was warm. "Because I wanted to give you pleasure. I wanted to watch your face. You were lovely," he whispered before kissing her lightly on the lips.

Morgana's body had quieted. She felt the relaxation that came with fulfillment. Tears pricked the back of her lids, and she wanted to say something as beautiful as Nicholas had just said to her. This was a new experience for her. Miles had been interested in her pleasure only occasionally and only insofar as it had reflected on *his* prowess as a great lover. He had lacked the sincerity she recognized in Nicholas, and it was up to her to return it in kind, Morgana thought as she ran her hands over her lover's body.

"But what about you?" she whispered, wondering how she could please him best.

"Don't worry about me. Worry about us." Nicholas rolled over onto his back, taking her with him, never breaking that most intimate of contacts. "Now we can watch each other."

"This time is for you," Morgana insisted as she began to move her hips in small circles. She was sated, she thought. She ran her hands along his ribs, gratified when he shuddered. He was damp from her, and his body was slightly slippery. She bent over and rubbed her stomach against his, keeping her breasts positioned so that they lightly stroked his chest. Her softened nipples reacted instantly. With their tightening came a renewed thrill of desire that shot through her like an electrical charge. Her eyes widened in surprise. Nicholas grinned.

He stroked her thighs, then cupped her buttocks so he could set their pace. *Painfully slow,* Morgana thought as he languorously moved her against him. Morgana felt herself drifting to that incredible world of color and heat that existed in her mind, but she was determined to take Nicholas with her this time.

Morgana kissed his chest, his shoulders, his neck, but somehow, Nicholas captured her lips with his. His mouth then followed the column of her neck, exciting her with soft bites. As they pleasured each other, Morgana fought for control, but when he suckled her breast, she was lost.

Her magic man had sent her to that otherworld filled with sexual sensation. But even as her eyes closed, she saw Nicholas with his silver gray gaze, his angular face, his challenging smile. Senses heightened, Morgana was aware of the scent of their sweat-slicked bodies, the lingering taste of salt she had licked from his skin. As his mouth continued to torment her deliciously, her fingers found and caressed the back of his neck. She heard his answering groan.

"Nicholas," she whispered as her inner world lit with burning colors.

He quickened their pace and lifted his head from her breast. "Morgana, love . . ."

She opened her eyes but lost none of the magic. In his face Morgana recognized more than passion. A kind of wonder was reflected there, as though he were seeing her for the first time.

"I think you've bewitched me," he whispered before a deep growl escaped him.

So he had joined her in their world of enchantment. Morgana covered his face with passionate kisses as he gripped her buttocks and pulled her hard against him. Their tremors came concurrently, not beginning small and growing, but hitting them with the full force of a cosmic explosion. They cried out together, and Morgana was somehow sure that Nicholas could see the flames that surrounded them. Slowly they flickered, then died.

Morgana lay still on top of Nicholas, her ear to his heart. When its beat stabilized to a normal pattern, she lifted her head. He was staring at her, but his eyes were a warm gray. He stroked the hair away from her face and kissed her gently.

"I think I like being an errant lady," she told him.

"Me, too," Nicholas said. "As long as I am your knight, you can be as errant as you like."

They laughed together, and Morgana thought it was a warm sound. "But if you keep spurning your food in favor of other pursuits, you will be too weak to carry me around," she told him with a smile.

"Food!" Nicholas said with enthusiasm.

"It's going to be cold," she warned.

"I don't care. I'm so hungry I could eat a . . . dragon!"

They laughed again as they hurriedly dressed and raced back to eat their cold steaks and potatoes. When they finished, they settled comfortably on the bench, Morgana leaning against Nicholas. They sipped their wine. The last orange and purple streaks of sunset faded and vanished across the lake. The hurricane candles remained unlit, for they were content with the darkness.

"Want to hear something funny?" Morgana whispered. "I thought *you* were the groom."

"What?" Nicholas pulled away slightly so he could face her. "You mean, you thought Mari and I . . . She's a little young for my taste, you know."

Morgana grinned. "I didn't find out differently until after our dinner date. When I stormed inside, I saw the invitation information in the office. I was stunned!"

"That's why you were so prickly." He chuckled. "I couldn't figure out why you wanted my little sister's approval. Waiting for you was worth it, though. I've never been seduced before. Why don't you do it again?"

Morgana thought about protesting. She really ought to tell him the truth, that she had seduced him only for a little personal attention and a kiss. But, then, why spoil his fun?

"You mean like this?" she murmured softly before slipping both her hands under his shirt and attacking him with her lips.

"Exactly!" came his muffled reply.

CHAPTER SIX

"Mr. and Mrs. Harry Balmoral accept. Ms. Karen Scofield and friend accept. Mr. and Mrs. Jonathan Murray decline. That's it," Nicholas said, shuffling the myriad invitation responses into neat piles.

Morgana quickly scanned the long list of guests. "Not bad. About two-thirds of the invitations have been returned, and there's a week to go before Mari's wedding. In view of how quickly this one was organized, it'll be a miracle if we hear from everyone by next Saturday. I'm amazed at the number of replies. It says something about how highly people think of you and Mari," Morgana said.

"I wouldn't know what was typical," Nicholas admitted. "Do you always take care of the responses?"

"Not really. Usually the task falls to the bride's mother."

"Well, Sondra isn't *usual* in any sense of the word," he said, referring to his and Mari's mother. "It doesn't surprise me that she and Walter won't be returning from Paris until Thursday."

"Tell me about her," Morgana urged, wanting to know everything about the man she'd grown so close to in the last two weeks. Nicholas had been reluctant to offer any more information than the fact that he and Mari had had different fathers.

Nicholas smiled at her, and Morgana impulsively touched

his warm lips. The first time they met in her shop they had seemed so hard and forbidding, she remembered. Nicholas caught her hand and kissed its palm.

"So you demand more information about Sondra and our relationship, do you?"

Morgana nodded. "I've answered dozens of questions about Blanche and our background and business. Now it's your turn. Fair's fair."

"I guess you're right. I don't have experience in sharing personal things with someone else. I need to learn how." Nicholas hesitated for a few seconds, his brow furrowed. "I'm fond of Sondra, but sometimes it's difficult to think of her as my mother."

"So you call her by name."

"Actually it was her request on my high school graduation. She's appalled to think people might guess her real age, you see. By the time I was halfway through college, *she* needed a parent figure. Mari's father died, and Sondra couldn't really cope until she found husband number four."

"Walter Steinberg is your mother's *fourth* husband?"

"Fifth. My mother was a hard woman to satisfy. My father didn't make enough money for her. Number two made it but didn't want her to spend it except as he dictated. Boarding school for me was Bart's favorite luxury," he said reminiscently.

As Nicholas spoke, he fumbled with Morgana's hand. Having grown to recognize the various nuances of his personality, Morgana realized how much it cost him to reveal the uncertainty of his childhood. She squeezed his hand reassuringly and was rewarded with a smile that warmed his eyes. How could she ever have thought them cold?

"Sondra truly loved Jacques DuMont. She stayed with

93

him, even after his business had failed. When he died, Jacques left her destitute."

"And you with a large responsibility."

"Twenty years old and I had a mother and a seven-year-old sister to support. It was then that I swore Mari would never want for money or love."

"It must have been hard on you."

"In some ways it was, but it made me stronger. Ambitious. Maybe even compassionate. I learned exactly how insecure Sondra was then. It was the only time in my life we were close." He grimaced. "It didn't last long. A few years later Sondra met number four and was off again. Martin was her richest husband. She could spend his money to her heart's content as long as she said nothing about his mistresses. He finally found someone younger and prettier he preferred to my mother."

"She must have been devastated."

Nicholas laughed. "I think she was relieved. And she rather enjoyed playing the martyr. Believe me, she took Martin for a bundle."

"Money isn't everything." Morgana sighed, wondering how Nicholas had risen above his childhood to become the terrific person he was.

"Wait a minute," Nicholas said chastisingly. "Here we've been talking about me when you have work to do. Or were you toying with me, fair maiden, when you swore you had too much work to go out tonight? Perchance you think to rid yourself of me and find some other knight more to your liking?"

He was glaring at her, making Morgana giggle. Yet there was a hint of seriousness behind his lighthearted banter. He couldn't really believe that, could he? In view of his past, perhaps he could. Morgana rushed into his arms to assure him.

"Oh, sir knight, I swear you tax my energy unduly. I have none left for some other poor knave. I am an errant lady in your arms only."

Nicholas kissed her then, neither softly nor seducingly but harshly, as though he were stamping her with a brand of his possession. He released her quickly, leaving Morgana breathless and wide-eyed.

"Now where's that work?" he asked.

"Let's start writing the names of your guests on these place cards."

They went to work in comfortable silence, but Morgana couldn't help asking, "What about Walter?"

Nicholas smiled at her indulgently. "Sondra met him a few years ago. I think she's genuinely fond of him, as he is of her. They seem comfortable together."

"I'm glad." Morgana was quiet for a moment before continuing. "Nicholas?"

"M-m-m?" He was concentrating on writing a place card.

"Is that why you never married? Because of Sondra?"

"Not at all. Instead, I learned the real values of marriage. Raising a sister and building a business didn't leave me much time for fun. I was probably too preoccupied to attract serious attention from the right woman. More than likely I hadn't met her yet."

There was something about the way his eyes flashed at her—containing humor, admiration, and something else she couldn't or wouldn't interpret—that made Morgana flush. Uncomfortable with the direction the conversation was taking, she quickly changed the subject.

"You've been a great deal of help with Mari's wedding," Morgana said. "I've been trying to figure out how you can

95

spend so much time away from your office. I thought you were a very busy man."

"Good managers know how to delegate. I've trained my ambitious assistant director to cover for me in all but the most pressing problems. She has the number here in case I'm needed desperately."

Morgana squirmed in her chair as the thought *I need you* formed in her mind.

"Besides, I've discovered what a busy woman *you are.* I'm helping you as much as I can out of self-defense. It's the only way I can spend time with my errant lady."

As thrilling as Nicholas's admission was, it frightened her. Morgana had learned Nicholas Bedford was a determined, if fair-minded, businessman who knew what he wanted and went after it. He was a fast mover who didn't let anyone stop him from a goal. Would he be any different in his personal relationships?

Although she was impulsive and spontaneous in most ways, Morgana would never allow herself to get serious about a man without careful deliberation. She'd made one mistake in a relationship by throwing in her heart and letting her head follow later. Miles Lord had used her innocence—both physically and spiritually, for she had always believed in the innate goodness of people—as he had used her talent.

Nicholas Bedford wouldn't use you like that, an inner voice whispered. *He's an honest man.*

Morgana Lawrence wanted to believe it with all her heart.

"I'm done with these," Nicholas said, breaking into her thoughts. "Are there more?"

"No. I'm on the last place card myself." Morgana wrote out the name with a flourish. "Finished! Now I have to work on one of the dresses for the twenties wedding. Carla

96

found two women to do the intricate beading I told you about. They've done two panels so I could construct one of the garments and get an approval before we go any further."

"Sounds like a good idea," Nicholas said, slipping behind her as she packed the cards.

"This bride is more demanding than any of the others I've worked with. And her mother is worse," she added, stopping her work and enjoying his warmth as he pressed up against her backside. How his body heat tempted her to forget work altogether! "Her mother keeps making changes. Clients can be difficult," she said breathlessly as his hands captured her hips.

"Some of us are *harder* than others," he murmured into her hair. Nicholas pulled Morgana even closer, leaving her no doubt as to his meaning before he turned her around.

"M-m-m. The kind of client I have to handle delicately," she said seductively.

"Or one you could let plunge into your work with you!"

Nicholas ran his lips along her hairline and ever so slowly traced a maze over her face, ending at her lips. His kiss was long and lingering yet demanded nothing more than the momentary pleasure he was offering her. Morgana swayed into him and slipped her arms around his neck, pulling him closer.

"M-m-m. Naughty wench," Nicholas whispered, nipping her lower lip. "Get back to work."

He gently slapped her buttocks, and Morgana pretended her dignity was wounded as she left the office and entered the workroom to find the material. She heard his chuckle follow her. "They have a name for lads like you!" she shouted.

"I'll see what I can do about finding matching white horses," Nicholas said as he joined her.

97

"I didn't think Barney's palfreys would give us quite so much trouble," Morgana admitted as she spread the material on her cutting table.

"Neither did I."

Morgana thought about how pleased she was with her design for the twenties dresses. They were made out of see-through chiffon with long, flowing sleeves. Morgana had planned satin slips of the same shade to be worn under the delicate gowns. When the bride's mother critically insisted each of the six maids should have her own design—both cut and beading—Morgana had been tempted to tear out her own hair. Instead, she convinced the bride to choose a different color for each maid and to approve a simple variation in the sleeve and neckline of her own off-white gown.

Tacking the sheer lavender chiffon to her cutting table, Morgana positioned her paper pattern carefully. The beaded pattern would begin simply at the bustline, becoming more complex below the waist. The hem of the knee-length dress would be almost solid with the sparkling bits of glass.

"Crabapple Stables? I'd like to rent two matching white horses for next Saturday."

Morgana could hear Nicholas on the office phone while she worked. His nearness gave her a warm feeling as though she'd sipped a snifter of brandy.

"No such thing as a white horse? Ah-ha!" He paused. "Well, do you have two creams or two grays?" he asked. "Not two that match. All right. Thank you."

Morgana cut out the gown, entranced by the smooth, deep voice filtering through the doorway. Nicholas Bedford had a way of making her day, she thought. He'd really accomplished a large share of the tasks involved with Mari's wedding. Getting over her initial nervousness at involving romance and work, Morgana admitted it was nice to have a shoulder to lean on, especially one as strong as his. Not having to do all the paper work, make all the contacts, and follow up on the various details her partner should be doing was a real relief.

Now if only she could find a way to make Blanche take over those duties once the medieval wedding was over . . .

As a string of beads popped, scattering bits of glass all over the floor, Blanche's irresponsibility and grand promises to clients without regard for her feelings came home to Morgana vividly. *Damn! Blanche, you'd be in trouble if only I could work magic!*

Fantasizing, Morgana saw her sister chained to one of the worktables. For once Blanche's hair was not perfectly coiffed. A long strand hung in her eyes. Blanche sobbed as each of her perfectly manicured fingernails snapped down to the quick while she beaded row after row, yard after yard of delicate chiffon material.

The vision was so incredibly real that Morgana began to laugh hysterically.

"Is this one of your private daydreams, or can anyone join in?"

"Oh, Nicholas!" Morgana wiped the moisture from around her eyes. "You startled me. How did you know my imagination was working overtime?"

"I guess I'm just clever that way," he said teasingly, coming toward her. Suddenly he lost his footing and caught himself on the edge of the cutting table.

"The beads!" Morgana shouted, horrified that he might fall on a broken piece of the glass beads and hurt himself. Getting down on her knees to gather the dangerous glass bits from the floor, she told Nicholas about her fantasy.

"Blanche working?" he asked as he stooped to help her. "That is pretty funny."

99

Morgana realized there was no humor in his voice.

"I say, anyone here?" Barney's booming was accompanied by a light, tinkling sound.

Making the mistake of trying to rise at once, Morgana and Nicholas knocked heads.

"Ouch!"

"Oh, my, I didn't mean to interrupt anything, darlings," Barney told them as they peered over the top of the cutting table. "But really, on the floor? Tch-tch."

"A string of beads popped off the material, and we were trying to pick them up," Morgana said quickly before he could go on. Realizing how strange they must look on their knees, peeking out at him, she had to swallow a giggle.

"No need to explain to *me.*"

Barney was moving toward them and making that strange tinkling noise. Morgana stared at the wide embroidered band casually slung over his sweat shirt. Little glints of silver undulated against his chest.

"Barney, why in the world are you covered with bells?"

"Ah, I thought you'd never ask." Nicholas rose, helping Morgana to her feet as Barney explained. "In my usual thirst for authenticity I have delved into the costuming of the Middle Ages, absorbing details meticulously. There was a period of time when men and women decorated their clothing with bells. Tunics, belts, embroidery—they all were covered with the whimsical objects. Of course, the fad lasted for only about thirty years, so I suppose using them isn't a must."

"If you don't mind"—Morgana laughed—"we'll pass on this one."

"We don't want to wake any guests who might decide to nap during the ceremony," Nicholas said gravely.

"Jest on," Barney said, tinkling as he hopped up on a

counter. "You'll need a giggle when I tell you the most dreadful news!"

"What?" Morgana envisioned a dozen catastrophes. Had the troubadour lost his voice? Or had the fair been closed by the police for not having a license?

"The caterer has said an upright swan cake is an impossibility! He can't manage to make the proud neck arch."

Morgana breathed again. "Is that all?"

"All? All! Morgana, darling, do you realize how ridiculous our swan would look with its neck stretched out the length of the table? People will say it has drunk too much mead."

Barney sighed, and Morgana tried to keep her face properly sober. "Well, maybe he can use some kind of support inside."

"I suggested he use a stuffed swan's neck and head, but the unimaginative oaf called me a fool!" Barney mourned. "He insisted the guests wouldn't appreciate the feathers in their frosting."

"What about papier-mâché?" Nicholas suggested. When Barney perked up, Nicholas found a piece of paper and a pencil and sketched. "It could be a kind of support for the cake if the head, neck, and wings were connected. If they were covered with frosting, they would look like part of the cake."

Barney tinkled to his side. "Why, Bedford, I think you may be a bit of a genius!" Barney took the sketch from him. "Not bad at all. Maybe *you* should go into the wedding business." He waved the piece of paper around in the air. "I'm off to devastate that pompous ass of a caterer with *our* idea!"

As Barney made his melodious way out the door, Nicholas and Morgana burst out laughing, falling into each other's arms.

"Are you sure you didn't invent *him?*"

"Barney? He's an original."

"And so are you," Nicholas told her, kissing the tip of her nose.

Content to stay in the shelter of his arms for the rest of the evening, Morgana knew they should get back to work.

"Hold me like this much longer"—she sighed—"and the dress won't get sewn tonight."

"Does it absolutely need to be?"

"I really should do it, but now I'll have to repair the beading first. Who knows how long it'll take!"

"We could take a break from the grueling day. You know, sort of rest up and then go back to work."

The invitation in his voice and in his roaming hands began to seduce her from thoughts of business. She made a last, halfhearted try. "And then there's the matter of finding two matching gray or cream horses . . ."

"Taken care of."

"When?"

Nicholas chuckled at her surprise and ran his hands along her buttocks. "Probably when you were having your wild dream about Blanche's working! I should have thought of it before." A bold hand slipped up her side to her breast. "One of my best clients raises Arab stallions as a hobby." He was playing with her nipple through the light fabric of her blouse. "I figured he'd know where we could rent our matching nags."

"And he did?" Hope burned in her breast—or was it his fingers?—that they might be able to go upstairs. For a short break, of course.

"Uh-huh." The hand slipped down to trail over her stomach. "He's lending us two of his own."

"Oh, Nicholas, that's wonderful!" Morgana practically strangled him in her enthusiasm. *"You're* wonderful!"

She kissed him soundly, letting him know exactly how effective his sly seduction had been. Pressing against him, she moved her hips back and forth until she thought he would choke.

"To hell with work!" he growled, lifting her in his arms and heading for the stairs in spite of her protests that he would give himself a hernia and there they would be without any *means* to have fun for weeks and weeks. . . .

Resentfully Morgana awoke from the most wonderful dream! Nicholas had been holding her as though he'd never let her go, murmuring vows of love between passion-filled kisses he lathered over her body.

And then she was sure she'd heard a car door slam.

Had he gone? Morgana slipped out of bed and skimmed the length of the room to look out the front window. Moving aside the macramé hanger, she peeked through the leaves of her spider plant. Blanche had arrived. Her Mercedes stood sentinel at the curb.

On Saturday? Will wonders never cease! A quick glance at the antique grandfather clock, and Morgana's sleep-filled eyes popped open. *Nine in the morning?*

Yawning, Morgana padded back across the shining oak floor, greeting each of her myriad plants with a cheery note. She headed for one of her three dressmaker's dummies gracing otherwise barren corners of her single-room living area. Her robe was on the one next to the brass bed. Too bad antiques didn't come in king-size, she thought, dreamily remembering the long, long night.

Tying her robe, Morgana hugged herself and asked the dummy, "How do you know when you're in love?"

The question almost startled her except she'd been aware of its lurking in the cobwebs of her mind for the last week. Nicholas had turned out to be so different from what she had at first assumed. Perhaps in his own office, decked out in one of the three-piece suits that still gave her the shivers, he was the banker she had suspected him to be. But with her, well, he was . . . Nicholas.

Steady, patient, trustworthy, full of humor, passion, and infinite kindness. That was her Nicholas.

"My Nicholas," she whispered, trying out the words. They sounded right.

Why, he hadn't even blinked an eye when he first saw her living space! There were two small bedrooms now turned into storage areas, their heavy oak doors always closed. Since Morgana preferred to live with space and light around her, she'd had the connecting walls between the old living room, dining room, and kitchen torn out.

The results had pleased her tremendously. There was room to spare after she had loaded the area with her antique sideboard with the hidden stereo; the massive buffet, now filled with antique and modern wedding accessories, souvenirs, and other bric-a-brac; and the seating area of modern sectional pieces she could arrange and rearrange to her heart's content. All that separated the kitchen area from the rest was a breakfast bar with two high padded stools.

After sailing past them, Morgana descended the stairs, her feet bare. Voices came from the office. She smiled. Nicholas *hadn't* left. Blanche's conversation with him wafted through the open doorway, but their words barely registered on Morgana.

"After I discussed this with Evan, we agreed your professional advice would be welcome, Nicholas. Your business reputation is outstanding."

"Are you sure you wouldn't be more comfortable consulting someone else? After all, I'm not exactly a disinterested party."

Not feeling a bit guilty that she hadn't gone back downstairs to work on the twenties dress the previous evening, Morgana paused at the cutting table. She might as well assess the damage now.

"I'm sure you wouldn't let it interfere. Really my husband is absolutely *desperate* to find a more suitable business venture."

"And he wants to do this immediately?"

Relieved to find the beading had popped almost entirely from the seam area, Morgana shifted her attention to her sister's words.

"Yes! Evan has been worried about the financial considerations for some time now."

What was Blanche talking about? Morgana wondered. It sounded as if Evan's business were in trouble. And her sister hadn't said a thing to her. No wonder Blanche had been so distracted from Fantasy Weddings lately. How could she keep her mind on her work here when she was worried about her husband and his business?

Remembering the fantasy she'd had about chaining Blanche to a worktable, Morgana experienced a sharp pang of remorse. Maybe there was something *she* could do to help, Morgana thought, rushing to the office to comfort her distraught sister.

"Let me think about it, Blanche," Nicholas was saying. "Perhaps there *is* a way out of this problem."

"Oh, thank you, Nicholas! I *knew* I could count on you!"

"Blanche—"

"Morgana!" Blanche jumped. Turning, she stared at her younger sister, wide-eyed. "I didn't know you were there. I came in to pick up a folder. Now where is it?"

Blanche was acting strange, Morgana thought, watching the well-dressed woman scurry around the office! She sighed, realizing Blanche wasn't about to confide in her today. How noble! She didn't want Morgana to worry, too.

"Oh, there it is!" Blanche snatched a folder from one of the shelves.

"Blanche . . ." Morgana tried again.

"Oh, darling, I can't stop to chat. I've got an appointment in fifteen minutes," she called over her shoulder, already rushing out the door.

When Blanche was gone, Morgana turned to Nicholas, wondering if she should quiz him. No, it wouldn't be right. Blanche had confided in him, and Morgana wouldn't urge him to break the trust.

"Sleep well?" he asked.

"Wonderfully. I'm ready to face anything today."

Morgana stepped into his arms, and Nicholas kissed her lingeringly.

"I've some urgent business of my own to attend to."

"Then you're leaving me," she said with a sigh.

"With regrets," he said assuringly, then kissed her once more. "But I'll be back tonight if you want."

"I want."

Morgana escorted her lover to the door. One last passion-filled kiss, and he was gone. She was left alone to think about her sister's problems. Where had their old relationship gone? she wondered. As teen-agers they had shared everything. Morgana was sure Blanche would confide in her eventually. She would do anything in her power to help. Of course, the situation might not be as serious as it had sounded. Blanche did have a way of exaggerating things.

Shaking her head, Morgana headed for her workroom. Idle speculation wouldn't get her anywhere. She had a full day of work ahead of her.

CHAPTER SEVEN

Romance is my joy,
And my love the finest.
I'll be true to her,
As long as the sun lights the sky.

The troubadour accompanied his song with the strumming of his lute. Clothed in scarlet and purple, he had enthralled the wedding guests until the arrival of the bride and groom.

"Oh, she looks like a fairy princess!" a woman cried.

Standing among the guests in front of the marriage tent, Morgana strained to catch a better glimpse of Mariette. She had seen the cream silk dress many times before, but the effect of the slight figure mounted sidesaddle on the pale steed was indeed magical. The sun glinted off the gold embroidery on Mari's brocade overtunic. The short blond curls beneath her veil and circlet seemed to be made of the same precious material.

I'm very happy, for the one
Whose love I seek's so beautiful . . .

The song continued as Mariette dismounted, aided by her maid of honor and Nicholas. Although the crowd oohed and ahed over Mari's costume, Morgana couldn't help focusing on the tall figure of her brother. His tunic of silver and blue seemed to emphasize the elegance of his features. When Nicholas turned toward the crowd and smiled warmly, Morgana knew he was looking directly at her.

"Who gives away the bride?" the minister asked from the tent entrance.

"I do," answered Nicholas, approaching with Mariette on his arm.

Christopher Paige, the groom, stood to one side of the minister. He, too, had arrived on horseback, but from the opposite direction.

Morgana was amazed once again when she saw the groom. With his blond curls, blue eyes, and youthful face, Christopher looked more like Mariette's brother than Nicholas did. Standing only a half head taller than his bride, dressed in the same colors of cream with gold and blue, Christopher was a fairy-tale prince worthy of his princess.

Morgana's eyes were still on Nicholas as the bridal pair followed medieval custom. They pledged their troth and exchanged rings outside the marriage tent, then entered.

As the guests filed inside the tent pavilion, the troubadour explained in a musical voice, "The word 'wedding' comes from the old English term wedd, or pledge, dating from medieval times."

Morgana seated herself on a folding chair under the canopy and glanced around. She noted in the front row the bleached blond head that was sure to belong to Sondra, Nicholas and Mariette's mother. Morgana spotted Blanche and her husband farther back, wedged between some guests who had dressed themselves in medieval garb. Blanche had not bothered to put together a costume, but she was wearing her North Shore best. Morgana knew her sister would be sure to attend *this* wedding, teeming as it was with socialites

109

and other notables who were friends or acquaintances of the Bedford/DuMont/Steinberg family.

"Christopher Paige, do you take this woman to be your wife?" the minister began.

The bride and groom held right hands as they stood before the assemblage. Across the rows of seated guests Nicholas's eyes met Morgana's.

Throughout the ceremony Morgana was distracted by her own thoughts. Although things were going well, there were still several last-minute tasks before the guests sat down to the feast.

Shortly before the ritual ended, Morgana slipped away to attend to her duties. Afterward she couldn't find Nicholas. The bridal party had not yet joined the multitude seated at rustic tables under the reception canopy.

"Two hundred people!" Sondra Steinberg exclaimed to Morgana, waving one ringed hand for emphasis. "What a lot of work you girls have done."

"Yes," said Morgana, thinking wryly of Blanche's "work."

"I wish I could have been in the States a few weeks earlier. I would have helped. I have a creative bent too, you know. Unfortunately"—Sondra sighed, blinking her false eyelashes—"La France is so busy in the summer. And Walter knows so many people with so much money. The parties! It was *très difficile!* Oh, do you speak French?"

"A little," Morgana admitted.

"Please excuse me, my dear. I tend to lapse into it. It's my second language, you know. Hello, hello, darlings!" Sondra struck a pose and waved to a couple entering the food pavilion.

Wasted theatrics, Morgana thought. It would be difficult to miss Sondra. Mari's mother wore a crimson silk shantung suit, featuring a narrow slit skirt that showed her petite figure to advantage. Sondra was quite attractive, Morgana thought, an older *femme fatale* version of Mariette.

"I love the French designers, don't you? I once thought I'd be a designer myself, but I got so busy. I've been married and married and married. Oh, *l'amour!*" A frown creased Sondra's carefully made-up face as she stared at her empty glass. "Walter? Could you bring me some more wine?"

Her husband, a distinguished-looking man in his fifties, dutifully procured a glass of spiced wine for her.

"Walter, you've met Morgana, one of the girls who own Fantasy Weddings?"

Her teeth on edge at the term applied to her, Morgana dutifully extended her hand. She thought she'd met Walter earlier, but she couldn't be sure.

"I have to check things over," Morgana told them. "Please excuse me."

Morgana left the Steinbergs. It was a relief to escape Sondra's effervescent presence. How could Nicholas and Mariette have become the people they were with such a shallow mother? she wondered.

There *had* to be more to Sondra, Morgana thought, chiding herself. She shouldn't be so critical. Sondra was merely an example of an unusual social set. Morgana knew she'd have to deal with its members again in view of the nature of her profession.

Morgana moved among the banquet tables, watching guests help themselves to roast beef, cornish pies, chicken, meat fritters, venison, various breads, jellies, salad, and fruit. The unique swan cake sat on a table at the head of the pavilion, surrounded by little honey cakes and bowls of spiced wine punch. Nicholas's idea had worked perfectly.

"Morgana!"

Larry and Sharon Matthews beckoned to her. "What a stunning dress! I'm sure you designed it yourself," Sharon commented. "You're always in step with the themes of your weddings."

"Thank you." Morgana *had* designed and made her dress, a floor-length blue linen with bell skirt and tight bodice slashed to show a blue print undertunic. She had added a silver metal net to hold back her thick hair and belted the gown with a low-slung silver girdle.

"Have you seen Nicholas?" Morgana asked the couple.

"I think he's with the bride and groom having photographs taken," said Larry.

Of course. Morgana herself had arranged for the photographer. The bridal party was probably in the wooded area nearby.

As Morgana wound her way between the crowded benches, she saw Barney talking with some actors. He was wearing his Robin Hood hat, a green tunic hung with bells, and tights that bagged at the knees. In charge of entertainment, Barney was to see that performances ran smoothly. Some costumed actors infiltrated the crowd of guests; there were musicians walking about and the actress playing sorceress Morgan le Fay was reading palms. Announced by the troubadour, other performers entertained at the front of the pavilion. A colorful juggler was balancing oranges near the cake table.

Looking toward a copse of trees, Morgana saw Mariette and Christopher emerge hand in hand. But there was no Nicholas.

"Mariette?"

"We've just finished the photographs." Mari's sweet voice was warm. "They're going to be lovely, just like the wedding." Mariette took both of Morgana's hands. "I'm so

112

happy." As she embraced the taller woman, Mari whispered, "I hope you'll be happy, too."

"I *am* happy."

"But sometimes it takes *two* to get the most out of life," Mariette said. "Nicholas has something to ask you. He told me you wanted *my* approval."

A thrill ran through Morgana. Was Nicholas planning to propose to her? The thought made her lose track of the present. Mariette and Christopher had left her to take their places at the head table. There were cheers and a toast announced for the bride and groom.

Where *was* Nicholas? As Morgana searched the feast once more, she saw Sondra Steinberg madly batting her eyelashes at an attractive man. Morgana assumed Walter overlooked his wife's flirtatiousness.

A group of guests rose to follow an actor who led them in a medieval round dance. The movement in the crowded area threw Morgana to one side, and she caught sight of Blanche seated next to a mutual acquaintance. Separated by the table vacated by departing guests, Morgana could hear her sister's modulated voice.

"Yes. We're investing in a new business, a North Shore boutique. Evan thinks it will be much more profitable."

What was Blanche talking about? Had Evan found a way out of his financial difficulties? Watching her sister, Morgana was somehow reminded of Sondra Steinberg. Was it the designer suit?

"Blanche is *not* like that," Morgana said out loud, then looked to see if anyone had heard her. The sister she'd grown up with had changed in the past few years, but Morgana *knew* Blanche had good intentions at heart.

"Fantasy Weddings is much too much work," Blanche said complainingly.

113

Now Morgana grew angry. Blanche was revealing their internal problems to an outsider. She loved her sister, but Morgana would have to talk to her about this.

"And what art thou up to, my sexy lady?"

The husky voice was familiar, as were the strong hands gripping her waist. Nicholas drew Morgana back against his chest, nibbling her neck and ears hungrily.

"What art *thou* up to? I've been looking for you . . . thee for hours."

"Surely not that long." Nicholas turned Morgana in his arms. "I'll have to make up for it." Their lips blended in an intimate kiss. Morgana didn't care if people watched them. "I have a gift for my lady."

"I know," whispered Morgana, pressing her hips against him discreetly. "But don't you think we should wait until we get back to your town house?"

"For *that,* yes. For now, how about champagne?" Nicholas produced a bottle he had set on the table. "It's still cold. I got it from a cooler in my car so we could celebrate this wedding properly."

"How romantic!" Morgana exclaimed as Nicholas popped the cork. "I love champagne!"

Sipping the frothy liquid, Nicholas continued. "Consider this a precelebration. I have a proposition for you." His eyes raked Morgana's body.

Was this another erotic innuendo or a hint at a marriage proposal? she wondered.

"Why don't we leave this party and have one of our own?"

She protested, "I can't leave. It's my job to be here."

"Consider me your employer," he said insistently. "If I don't mind, why should you? Besides, I talked to Barney,

114

and he's promised to stay and take charge. It's time he took more responsibility."

Morgana was still unsure it was a good idea, but she let Nicholas lead her outside the canopy.

The troubadour was singing again:

I have to end this tune now
For I've had enough of song
And feast and dance. Come love, I'll never
Have enough of you.

"See?" said Nicholas. "Even he thinks we should leave the scene."

Morgana sat close to Nicholas during the ride back to the city. Relieved that he offered no more information about his important proposition, Morgana didn't press him. She was lost in her thoughts.

Her churning emotions matched the changing summer sky, now sunless and threatening. Although she'd known Nicholas for only five weeks, Morgana was certain she loved him. But was she ready to commit herself to marriage? Unsure, Morgana worried that their relationship would be ruined if she asked for more time. Unconsciously she stroked the brocade-covered thigh next to her own.

"Do you like me in this outfit?"

"The tunic becomes you, and you turn a well-shaped leg, milord," she said, running her hand *under* the tunic. "You fill out your tights nicely."

"I'll look even better without them," Nicholas assured her, referring to their evening ahead.

Making an effort at lightheartedness, she replied, "Your conceit grows, milord."

"Along with other things," he muttered. Nicholas ran one

115

of his long-fingered hands down her leg. "I'd prefer you with a little less clothing, too."

As they drove on, the comfortable silence between them stretched into something foreboding. Morgana grew aware of a brooding tension building within her as if her mood were reflecting the darkening sky ahead. Nervously glancing at the man beside her, she saw a stranger.

Curse her imagination! She loved Nicholas, and there was nothing he could say to her so frightening as to alienate her like this. Seeking his warmth and reassurance, Morgana moved closer to him. Nicholas put his arm around her.

"Storm's coming up."

"I hope this weather doesn't ruin Mari's reception," Morgana said. "It's a good thing we invested in tents."

Nicholas turned on his headlights. A bank of ominous black clouds gathered to the east as they neared his town house complex. A moment later he parked at the curb, not able to get into his driveway because Morgana's car filled it.

"We'd better hurry," he told her.

By the time she pushed open her door against the ferocious wind, Nicholas was at her side helping her out. With one hand Morgana shielded her eyes against the particles of dust beating at them. She held her swirling skirts with the other. The first gust of cold rain made her shiver.

"Don't worry." Nicholas drew her close to him. "I'll get you inside quickly." As he inserted his key in the lock, he was singing slightly off-key, "What do I care? I've got my love to keep me warm."

"Do a tunic and tights always have this effect on you?"

"Don't know. If you think so, I intend to wear them more often."

Morgana wished she could match his humorous mood.

She would have to nip her ridiculous fright and believe everything would turn out all right.

Once inside, Nicholas took her in his arms. "Finally," he growled as his mouth closed over hers.

The kiss was searching and deep. Morgana forgot her worries as she eagerly responded. Her tongue pushed back at the delicious intruder in her mouth.

Nicholas ran his hands up her sides, cupping the outside of her breasts. Her nipples hardened, and she felt sweet fire spreading up from between her thighs.

"Let's go upstairs." He walked her backward, half carrying her to the stairway. "I want to make love to thee in my chamber. This knight is tired of hard castle floors."

For once Morgana's imagination failed her. She saw Nicholas as himself. She couldn't envision knights. The man who led her up the staircase and laid her gently on his bed was real. His solid presence bound her to the earth, not allowing her to experience her usual flights of fancy.

When they had shed their clothing, Nicholas lay next to her. She felt his heart beat against her breast. Their lips blended as she ran her hands over his firm flesh and felt his own cover her breasts in response.

"Um-m-m, nice," he murmured between caresses, inserting a knee between her thighs.

Morgana wanted no visions this night. She wished only that their flesh could melt—Nicholas's against her own. So vulnerable, even it was too solid to appease her. She needed to join with her lover, flesh searing, spirits melding. Pulling him to her, she cried out as Nicholas entered her body and slipped even more deeply into her core.

For tonight, more than ever, Nicholas became part of her very soul. When he murmured sweet assurances into her

117

hair, touching her with the hands of love, Morgana savored the reassurance she desperately craved.

This was no stranger but her Nicholas, the man she adored.

A flash of lightning flared through the room, allowing her to search the features she loved so well. There was such intensity reflected in them that Morgana grew doubtful once more. But a single touch of her fingers to his cheek elicited the groan of her name through his lips, quieting her anxieties.

As quickly as the storm had risen, so had the height of their passion. Volatile emotions merged with physical pleasure and writhed within Morgana. Her climb to release was short and intense, no more so than his. Morgana shuddered as the tension drained from her in wave after wave of fulfillment. She collapsed beneath Nicholas, his weight above her reassuring.

The storm outside had subsided somewhat. The beat of rain against the windows sounded much like that of her own heart.

"My most beautiful and wondrous lady," Nicholas whispered.

Morgana answered him with a tender kiss. They nibbled each other gently as the wind from the storm gently rocked the sliding glass doors. Unaware of time passing as they lay in the darkened room, Morgana was content. She started to doze.

"Morgana?" Nicholas queried, his voice awakening her instantly. "I have a surprise for you, sweetheart. Are you asleep?"

She opened her eyes. The light was dim, but she could make out his face. "What?" she whispered, smoothing the silvered hair at his temples. She was no longer afraid.

"After careful thought, and analyzing the situation you've been dealing with . . ."

As he hesitated, Morgana could feel his suppressed excitement. She wanted to share it. "Yes, Nicholas?"

"I know you'll be pleased. I've decided to become your business partner."

Morgana was stunned, barely listening to the rest.

"Blanche was anxious to sell me her half of Fantasy Weddings. We had the papers drawn up," he went on. "They lack only your signature."

Morgana couldn't breathe. A shadow from the past haunted her. Miles Lord entered her thoughts and lingered. Her mouth went dry, but she forced herself to speak. "Blanche sold out?"

"Yes. She offered to sell her half of the business to me last week," he said, stroking the side of her face. "I knew you'd be happy. And it's a good investment for me. I think I can make Fantasy Weddings show a healthier profit. If not, I'm an expert on tax losses. Besides, we'll be great working together. It'll be fun."

Morgana stared into the dark, listening to the storm outside. Once more it crashed around the town house, making the windows and doors shudder under the onslaught. Her world had collapsed around her and he thought they'd have fun?

"You're my new business partner. *That's* your proposal?" she said quietly, barely holding on to her composure. "Everything is arranged. I have nothing to say about it."

"Well, it's up to you to sign." Caution finally edged his voice. "I promise you won't be sorry, darling. I really thought you'd be pleased."

Morgana's emotions reeled. Blanche had sold her out.

Nicholas thought she could be bought like stock in some business merger. And that was supposed to please her!

"Get away from me!" Morgana fiercely pushed him to the side of the bed. Miles had used her for her talent, holding a contract over her head. Now Nicholas wanted to do the same. She bounded from the bed.

"Morgana, wait a minute. You can't go like this!"

"Watch me!"

"But I haven't finished."

"I've heard enough, Nicholas Bedford!" After switching on the overhead light, Morgana quickly riffled through the pile of clothing on the floor. "I can't believe you did this to me! I thought you were an honest man. I trusted you!"

"Morgana, if you'll calm down, I have something more to say!"

Her head snapped up at his stiff tone. What did *he* have to be upset about? She fumed. "This is yours!" she shouted, flinging his brocade tunic in his face, then quickly donned her gown.

"You're not looking at this logically," Nicholas insisted, practically vaulting out of the bed.

"Did you plan to buy my sister's half of the business behind my back or not, Nicholas?" Morgana demanded.

"Yes, technically, I guess I did, but I also wanted—"

But she was already out the bedroom door, heading down the stairs. She turned at the landing. "So you've bought my business! Well, it'll be a cold day in hell when you get to run it!"

Fleeing barefoot, Morgana opened the town house door into the full force of the storm. Her teeth chattered with cold and suppressed sobs as she struggled to open her car door. The driving rain matted her hair around her face, and rivulets of water seeped down her back. The strong wind buffeted her body against the vehicle as she managed to enter it. Once inside, bare, wet feet on the cold floor mat, Morgana leaned on the steering wheel and wept.

How could she have trusted Nicholas so blindly? He desired her business, not her. Another man who thought he could make money from her talent! Hadn't Miles been enough?

And Blanche . . . her own sister had instigated the betrayal.

Starting the engine, Morgana drove down the deserted, storm-ravaged streets, her tears blending with the rain on the windshield to blur her vision.

She was alone in a world of pain and darkness.

CHAPTER EIGHT

"How dare you, Blanche! I still can't believe it!"

"Morgana, be *reasonable,*" Blanche pleaded, nervously
pulling her long plum-colored fingernails across her forehead. "We both know you do more than half of the work.
Nicholas would make a better business partner than I."

Pacing the office while her sister sat, Morgana repressed
the urge to shake Blanche.

"That's not what we're talking about here, and you know
it! You're my own sister, and you couldn't be honest with
me." Morgana had gone over and over it all night, but it still
didn't make sense to her. Not if Blanche had any sisterly
feelings. "You never even hinted you wanted out of the business. And then you went behind my back and betrayed me!"

"You had enough on your mind," Blanche insisted. "I
didn't want to upset you with something more to worry
about until I'd come up with some kind of solution."

Morgana laughed at that. "You didn't want to *upset* me?
What a joke! I never thought you were so insensitive. My
own sister sells me out, and she doesn't think that's going to
upset me." Morgana felt tears starting, but she wouldn't cry
in front of Blanche. Taking a ragged breath, Morgana cut
off her sister before Blanche could get in a response. "Fantasy Weddings was *your* idea. *You* talked *me* into being your

partner. Tell me something, Blanche. Whatever possessed you to consider a business like this?"

"I guess because I envied you."

"What!" Morgana stared at her impeccably dressed sister, who was wringing her hands and biting her lower lip like a schoolgirl.

Blanche glanced up, and Morgana thought her sister's eyes were swimming with unshed tears. "You were always so ambitious. So creative. Mother and Father were always going on and on about their talented daughter Morgana."

"Don't be ridiculous. I had to fight them every step of the way to go to school at the Chicago Art Institute. Or have you forgotten?"

"I remember. They were proud of that, too. They expected it of you. You had strength and determination and made your own life. They didn't expect anything of me but to follow Mother's example and find a successful husband to support me. While I was having my children—a very ordinary accomplishment—you were winning awards for your costume designs."

"Yes, and while you were living in a grand house on the North Shore, I was sharing a two-bedroom apartment with secondhand furniture. Your pin money was more than the salary I earned and had to live on," Morgana protested, amazed at her sister's words. How often had her mother wished that Morgana could be more like Blanche? "You were envious of *me?*"

"Yes, Morgana. Then I decided that if I really put my mind to it, I could be as successful as you. But I couldn't. Oh, I did well enough when I worked as a part-time wedding consultant for someone else, but then my responsibility was limited and my duties were cut-and-dried." Morgana heard a definite quiver in Blanche's voice as she went on.

"But here . . . you expected so much of me. I found I just didn't have it to give. I'm not creative and never will be. And I'm lousy at accounts and all the dreadfully boring paper work involved in my half of the job."

"What *did* you think your job would be, Blanche?"

"Socializing with clients. Making contacts. Bringing in new business, that sort of thing. But as Fantasy Weddings became successful and I was faced with work I couldn't handle, well, the whole thing blew up into a living nightmare for me. I couldn't even do the things I enjoyed. I know it wasn't fair," Blanche added quickly, "but I saw myself stuck here forever in spite of the fact that Evan had been urging me to sell to anyone who would buy it for the last six months. I couldn't do it because of *you.*"

Morgana had been quietly and politely listening to her sister explain her position, but this was too much. "So now it's *my* fault you've been unhappy!"

"No, Morgana. I never said that. It's my own fault, and now I've made myself even more miserable. If that's possible. I was trying to find a way to make us both happy, and I failed again. I can't do anything right," Blanche wailed. "I didn't mean to hurt you, Morgana. I didn't! You've got to believe me," she said, sobbing, tears breaking loose and rolling down her face. Pools of mascara gathered at her lashes, emphasizing the hazel color of her eyes.

"By the time I spoke to Nicholas I was desperate," Blanche continued. She fumbled in her handbag for a tissue. "It was obvious he cared for you. I knew he'd have your best interests at heart."

"Best interests?" Morgana repeated as Blanche blew her nose. "He couldn't possibly," she insisted, turning away from her sister, "because Nicholas Bedford has no heart!"

Blanche jumped up from her chair and grabbed Morgana

by the arm. In spite of her lesser size, she was able to spin her sister around to face her.

"You know it's not true. It's the hurt in you talking. When I realized how serious Nicholas was about you, I hoped he'd buy me out. Then he made the offer, and I was so happy! We both thought it was the perfect solution. Can't you see that? We wanted to surprise you. We had the details worked out, nothing for you to worry about. Poor Nicholas thought you'd be pleased."

"Pleased! I should be pleased to allow him a say in every aspect of my life? I won't allow another man to control my business."

"Nicholas isn't Miles, Morgana."

Morgana stared, openmouthed. So even Blanche had known about the way Miles Lord had used her.

And Nicholas Bedford had proved to be more like Miles than she had ever thought possible.

Miles had used her talent to build his own reputation as a theater impresario, enforcing the exclusivity clause in their working contract when she wanted to go into business with her sister. During the remaining four months of their contract, Miles had made life more and more miserable for her because she refused to renew.

Then, when Fantasy Weddings became a reality, he'd thrown her out with nothing, not even an unblemished professional reputation. In a magazine interview the following month, he'd taken credit for all her award-winning designs, claiming she'd only executed his ideas.

It was then she'd vowed to keep work and personal relationships as far apart as possible. How could she have forgotten and let Nicholas get close to her business by allowing him to help with Mariette's wedding?

125

Obviously she was still naïve. She hadn't learned anything from her experience with Miles.

Making a great effort to keep control, Morgana kept in her seething emotions. "I don't want to discuss Nicholas Bedford," she told her sister.

"All right, Morgana. Whatever you want. I'll do anything, but don't look at me that way. I'm not your enemy. I'm your sister."

"You should have thought of that yesterday, Blanche. You should have remembered before you sold me out." Morgana couldn't help it. A tear spilled out of each eye.

"Don't say it like that," Blanche pleaded. "It wasn't that way. We didn't . . . I didn't mean to hurt you. You do believe me, don't you? I admit I made a mistake, but I'll make it up to you. I *promise*. I'll tear up the contract and stay. All right? Is that what you want? I promise I'll try harder if you just forget about this incident."

Blanche blinked rapidly, and the pools of mascara left dark trails on her cheeks. "Please say you'll forgive me, Morgana. *Please.*"

Morgana pulled away, touched by her sister's apparent sincerity in spite of her determination to remain unaffected. But Morgana wondered how long Blanche's new resolve would last before she broke down once more.

Sighing, Morgana knew she'd forgive her sister. But she couldn't tell Blanche that. Not yet. The pain was still too fresh. Too sharp.

"Morgana, tell me what to do. What do you want me to do?"

"I don't know what I want, Blanche. I'll have to think about it. Give me some time."

"All right, Morgana." Blanche shuffled nervously and

blew her nose again. "I'll be going now." When Morgana didn't answer, she asked, "Shall I call you later?"

"No. I'll call *you* when I've made up my mind. It may take a few days."

"Good-bye," said a subdued Blanche, her shoulders drooping as she left the office.

Morgana waited to hear the outer door slam before she collapsed behind her desk. Covering her face with both hands, she took a deep, shuddering breath.

Obviously Blanche would never be a better partner than she already was. She'd gone into Fantasy Weddings because of a sense of inferiority. Rather than assuage those feelings, their business had increased them. Oh, Morgana was convinced her sister would try to do better just as she had promised.

For a while.

But eventually the guilt would grow into anger. Blanche would feel trapped and resentful, and her good intentions would dissolve as easily as they had been formed.

Then Morgana would be faced with running the firm herself once more. The situation could become intolerable.

Morgana couldn't even dislike her sister for what she had done. Instead, she felt sorry for her. Not for a moment, however, did she believe Blanche had planned to sell her half of the business secretly out of thoughtfulness for Morgana's feelings. She'd done it to spare *herself,* probably convinced her sister would be mildly upset yet relieved at the same time.

Nicholas Bedford was a different story. He had no excuse for doing this to her! From what she had gathered, he was an honest businessman, but she still didn't want him involved in her professional life.

His words on leaving his sister's wedding came back to haunt her: *Consider me your employer.*

"No wonder he demanded we leave the wedding without consulting anyone else," she muttered angrily. "He thought he already owned the business. Well, if he has any ideas about running it, he's got another thought coming!"

The significance of her words stunned her. Without realizing it, she was considering letting Blanche and Nicholas get away with their deceit.

"No! Never!" she cried.

But what alternatives did she have?

According to her contract with Blanche—one she had been foolish enough to let Evan draw up without consulting her own lawyer—either party could sell her half of the business. The other partner could object and find her own buyer —within thirty days. She knew Blanche didn't mean to press it now. But what if Evan should get to her and *demand* she go through with the sale? The money was really *his* after all.

And whom could she find to buy Blanche's half? Morgana didn't count many business people in her circle of friends. None, actually. And she herself couldn't afford to buy Blanche out. Could she take another loan? Morgana shuddered at the prospect of being inspected as though she were some strange species by the bankers who issued that kind of money. No, she couldn't subject herself to that kind of torture again.

It would serve them all right if she walked out on the business. But then she'd lose everything.

At least Miles had taken only her heart. If Blanche sold to Nicholas and Morgana walked out on *him,* he'd have everything she cared about. Evan had made sure he'd put that in the contract, too. She was in a no-win situation.

All day Morgana tried to work, but everything she put her hand to failed. Finally, she gave up, took a hot bath, and went to bed early. Sleep eluded her for most of the night, and she rose with the Monday morning sun.

She had come to a decision.

Now wanting to get the thing over with as soon as possible, Morgana counted down the minutes until nine o'clock, punctuating each half hour with at least one more cup of coffee. At nine exactly she breathed a sigh of relief and lifted the phone. With trembling fingers Morgana dialed his office number.

"Bedford and Associates" came the slightly nasal announcement.

"Mr. Bedford, please."

"I'm sorry, but he's not in at the moment. May I take a message?"

Morgana wasn't prepared to deal with the sterile voice of Nicholas Bedford's secretary. She'd been counting on his being at work on time. Pressing her fingers to her throbbing temples, Morgana instructed herself to remain calm.

"What time will Mr. Bedford be in?"

"I don't know, ma'am. May I take a message?"

Was the other woman stalling her? she wondered. That was ridiculous, for even if Nicholas had told his secretary he didn't want to speak to any Morgana Lawrence, she hadn't offered the woman her name.

Morgana patiently tried again. "Will he be in this morning?"

"I really don't know." The secretary's voice had gone from sterile to huffy when she asked for the third time, "May I take a message?"

Morgana lost her patience. "Well, do you know if he's at home?"

129

"No, he's not," the secretary practically shouted. "But I *can* take a message."

"No message."

After dropping the receiver back in its cradle, Morgana stared at the phone as though it, too, had betrayed her. Her nerves were stretched to the breaking point. Why did this have to be so difficult? she wondered. And where was Nicholas?

Trying to distract herself, Morgana decided to begin straightening out her supply cabinet—a job long overdue. It was a tall affair, so she had to use a stool to reach the top shelf. The cabinet overflowed with sewing supplies and notions, swatches of fabric, and samples of silk flowers, laces, appliqués, ribbons, and beading. Add to that leftovers of every wedding they had done, and the shelves bulged.

By the time it was half-empty Morgana was anxious to try again, so she approached the phone once more. This conversation was almost verbatim of the last, and the secretary was snippy all the way through.

She tried again later. Twice, in fact, but there was no Nicholas. His secretary became so agitated with her that she slammed down the phone right in the middle of Morgana's frustrated questions.

At precisely 10:18 Nicholas Bedford strode through the front door of Fantasy Weddings. Exactly as though he owned it, Morgana thought. Blanche must have given him the keys!

Standing on a stool, arms full of supplies meant for the top shelf, Morgana watched in horror as Nicholas came to rest before her. He was dressed in a three-piece pinstriped suit—one that *definitely* made her shudder—with a facial expression to match. There was no mistaking it. He was there on business.

"Good morning, Morgana. Is that how you're greeting your clients these days? Business will either improve greatly or die altogether."

His tone was wary; his attitude, reserved. And yet she almost felt his anger. Looking down at her toes, she saw them peeking out from under her nightgown—a very thin, sexy one at that!

Oh, God! she thought. Could this be happening to her on top of everything else?

"I am not open for business yet, Mr. Bedford."

Her voice was cool, yet her body felt like a coiled spring waiting to be released. She shifted, wondering what to do with her armload of notions, her only defense against his penetrating eyes. She had to get down off this stool sometime.

"If you're not open for business, then why is your door open?" he demanded frostily.

She hadn't left it open! Quickly she shoved the supplies away from her, but only half of them landed on the shelf. The rest dropped around her, and in her attempt to salvage them, she almost fell off the stool. Strong hands circled her waist and steadied her. Morgana felt her blood racing. Unwanted emotion surged through her.

"Let go of me!" she croaked, trying to nullify her response.

"I should have let you fall," he muttered, releasing her. "Why the hell is the door open when you're dressed like that?" he demanded.

"I didn't know it was open. Blanche!" Her sister must have left it open, and Morgana had been too upset to check it. "She was here yesterday."

"That door was left open all night?" he said, raging. "Do you know what could have happened?"

131

"Yes, something could have been stolen," she replied coldly. So he saw all this as his already, did he? She felt some of her carefully thought-out resolve slip away.

If she read him right, Nicholas was ready to strangle her. Yet he regained control easily enough, saying, "Yes, stolen. To say nothing of your personal safety."

"Oh!"

Morgana hadn't thought about that. He must feel something for her if he was concerned with her welfare. She wouldn't think about it, she told herself sternly. When she realized his eyes were glued to the skimpy lace top of her flesh-colored nightgown, Morgana looked around wildly, searching for something to use as a cover-up. Spotting a length of peach chiffon left over from the twenties wedding, she grabbed it and drew it around herself.

"Modest, Morgana? How unlike you," he said softly.

His cool words made her flush. And get angry.

"What do you want, Mr. Bedford?" Her voice could have frozen water.

"I've brought you the papers we spoke of on Saturday night," Nicholas informed her just as frostily.

He held them out to her, his arm and fingers stiff. He might have been referring to a newspaper or a stack of typing paper for all the emotion registering in him! Morgana fumed. She snatched them from his hand.

"Thank you," she said glacially.

"I thought you might like to rip them up yourself."

Quickly Morgana glanced up from the bill of sale. Had his tone softened? Was there just a touch of regret in his voice? No, she must be mistaken.

Morgana forced her gaze down once more as she said, "I have no intention of stopping you from buying out Blanche." His body seemed to thaw, she noted from the

132

corners of her eyes. "I'm quite willing to accept you as my business partner." He *did* take a half step toward her, stopping only when she added with emphasis, *"Mr. Bedford."*

Morgana wondered if he recognized the hurt in her eyes as she lifted them from the incriminating papers. Nicholas was in complete control, however, and Morgana had no idea of what he saw or of what he was thinking.

Was he happy now that he had what he wanted? she wondered. And what exactly was that?

Her business was doing well and could be lucrative, but not so much that a man like Nicholas would do anything to have it. And he must feel something for her, Morgana sensed. More than likely he was turned on by the amount of control he envisioned he'd have over her. The kind of control Miles had been so fond of exerting for the two years she'd stayed with him. *Not again,* she vowed silently. *If those are your plans, I'll cheat you yet, Nicholas Bedford. No man will ever control me again.*

Aloud she said, "I'll sign these sale papers with a few additions."

"What kinds of additions?"

"Terms stating the division of our duties."

"What?" he asked, frowning. "You mean a contract above the old one?"

"A very binding and specific contract," Morgana told him. "We can draw up the terms now, but I'll have my lawyer look over everything before I sign."

"Obviously you've given this a lot of thought. I'm surprised you haven't done it already," Nicholas grumbled.

"I believe in being up front," Morgana told him, squarely looking Nicholas in the eye. *"I* don't draw up contracts behind people's backs."

Nicholas stiffened, and with satisfaction Morgana noted the bright patches of color suffusing his face.

"You never let me finish my explanation, Morgana. Because of our personal relationship, I thought you'd be happy. I wouldn't have done it with anyone else."

"That's a comforting thought!" Morgana exploded.

"If you'd only let me explain, perhaps you would feel different!" Nicholas growled.

"*Nothing* you could say to me would make any difference. My business is the most important thing in my life! The *only* important thing," she added in amendment. "And I am willing to continue our association at that level."

"If it's business you want, then that's what you'll get," Nicholas said tersely.

He stared at her, and Morgana was confused by the quickly shuttered expression she glimpsed. Was it hurt? Knowing how it felt, Morgana was tempted to soften her attitude. But no, she wouldn't do it. She herself had been hurt enough by Nicholas and Blanche, and she wouldn't open herself up to more. She headed for the sanctuary of her office.

"We'll be more comfortable working at a desk, don't you agree?"

"Yes, and it certainly would be much more *businesslike.*"

Cringing at his tone, she didn't respond. Once ensconced behind her own desk, Morgana felt safer from him. She felt in control there, even dressed as she was in a thin nightgown and bolt of cloth. She shuffled papers around, giving herself time to approach the agreement calmly.

Nicholas didn't have to accept the addendum to the contract to buy out Blanche, and Morgana was sure he knew it. But unless he accepted her terms, she'd never sign the papers, and he'd wait another month to get an unwilling partner. *If* she didn't walk out on him after all.

"Where shall we begin?" he asked, his gray eyes hooded.

"I want the separation of duties to be spelled out. I will handle all the creative aspects of Fantasy Weddings, and you'll take care of the business end."

"Go on."

Drawing two columns on a piece of paper, her name topping one, his the other, Morgana wrote as she spoke.

"My main job will be to design and oversee the construction of wedding garments. In addition, I'll take the responsibility for the general staging and production of the wedding. That would include choosing the location, making arrangements with caterers and florists, and picking the entertainment."

Morgana looked up at him expectantly for his reaction, unconsciously admiring his clear-cut profile and the light brown hair with silver threads.

"And what do I get to pick?" he asked dryly. "The color of the paper the invoices will be printed on?"

"As I said," Morgana told him, willing herself to forget what might have been between them, "I'll be responsible for the creative aspects. You'll handle the business end. You will find clients for Fantasy Weddings. That may involve publicity. You'll handle the finances—billing clients, paying suppliers, and so on. Plus I would expect you to handle problems with difficult customers or vendors, acting as a public relations person."

"As you see fit, of course."

"Of course."

Morgana flushed under his scrutiny. She'd given him all the boring, unimaginative jobs she didn't want to deal with, and he knew it. What did he expect? Had he really thought

135

she'd welcome him as an equal partner in the creative decision making? Fat chance!

"I'll agree to your terms," Nicholas said, "but you'll have to accept mine." He grabbed the paper from her and began making his own notes. "If I'm to handle the finances, then that includes finding ways of cutting costs and improving profit margins."

Although she didn't like the thought of his making any of the rules, Morgana couldn't see the harm in this particular idea. Larger profits wouldn't be unwelcome. If she could save more money, she'd be able to buy out Nicholas all the sooner.

"Agreed," she said.

"Good. That means *you* will have to give me an accounting for all moneys spent."

Morgana hadn't thought about having to do so. Opening her mouth to object, she hadn't got out a word before he raced on.

"If I think a supplier is overcharging for a product or service, I'll find someone more reasonable."

Not able to find a problem with that, Morgana agreed again. "Fine."

"Wonderful. Then it's all settled. I'll need a set of keys."

Trying to get out of giving him a set, Morgana objected, "But my apartment is part of the premises. I don't have it locked off in any way."

"I know," he said, his grin suddenly wolfish. And there was a strange gleam in his eye when he asked, "How much rent do you pay Fantasy Weddings?"

"What?" He had to be kidding!

"Does that mean you haven't been paying rent this last year?" Nicholas asked, obviously enjoying finding a way to upset her calmly thought-out resolve.

136

"But I worked for this place, and you damn well know it, Nicholas Bedford!"

"Yes, but Blanche was your partner then, and don't forget I am not in the same league. You've been receiving a very nice side benefit of the business, but that will have to be reconciled. I'll research comparable rents in the area, and we'll negotiate," he told her, one eyebrow raised in challenge.

"You can't be serious!"

"Oh, but I am, Morgana. If you don't want to pay out the rent, we could make the apartment available to *both* owners. Either on a first-come, first-serve basis . . . or we could share—"

"Forget it!" Morgana couldn't believe the man's nerve. First he tried to steal her business; now he wanted her home, too.

"If you say so. We'll discuss the terms later then." Nicholas rose, obviously satisfied with himself. Smiling, he reminded her, "Don't forget the keys."

"Don't worry, Mr. Bedford, you'll get your damn keys!" Morgana told him, already planning to install a dead bolt on the door to her apartment.

Nicholas was already on his way out of the office. "Oh, and Morgana?" he said cheerfully.

"Yes?"

"Call me Nicholas." He whistled as he escaped to the front door.

"O-o-oh!"

Was he trying to wangle his way back into her private life? She'd show him she was no easy target! By the time she saved the money to buy him out Nicholas would be happy to sell. She had to stop feeling sorry for herself and concentrate on the future. Too bad she had no aptitude for revenge.

137

In a last moment of weakness Morgana closed her tired eyes and tried to pretend the horror of betrayal hadn't actually happened to her. *Pretend it's all a nightmare,* she thought. But once again Morgana's imagination failed her just as it had the last time Nicholas made love to her.

Was it one more thing Nicholas had taken from her? Morgana wondered sadly.

CHAPTER NINE

Entering Fantasy Weddings, Morgana slammed the door behind her, wondering why it had been unlocked. Was Nicholas here again, not having bothered to call? She froze. The sketches! Had she left them on her desk?

After racing through the reception area, she found Barney stretched out on the small office couch.

She blew a sigh of relief. "It's *you!*"

"Yes, 'tis I," Barney admitted, theatrical weariness in his tone. " 'Tis not the boogeyman Bedford."

"I asked him not to come here unless he called first."

"And has he respected your wishes?"

"So far." Until she began working with Nicholas, Morgana hadn't realized how much she regarded the office as an extension of her personal space. "Except for our two planned meetings a week, he has no reason to be here at all."

She examined the papers lying on her desk. The incriminating designs were on top of the pile. What a stupid place to put them, she chided herself. If Nicholas had come in rather than Barney, he might have discovered her secret.

Morgana plopped down beside Barney. "I'll tell you something if you promise not to breathe a word to Nicholas."

"Of course, my dear. Why would I tell that Philistine anything?"

Before Barney could launch into further exposition, Morgana confided, "We have a new client. Charlotte Claffey. I met her at the Matthews' Victorian wedding. She wants me to design Art Nouveau dresses for a November event." Handing him the sketches, she asked, "What do you think?"

"Quite striking, my dear!"

"I'm trying for a stained glass effect, using appliquéd and quilted yokes. I can use autumn colors since Charlotte doesn't like white."

Barney nodded, sitting up on the couch. He inspected the drawings, asking, "Why don't you want the infamous Bedford to know about this?"

"Because I'm tired of his intervention and small-mindedness," Morgana stated vehemently. "He thought I should have used cheaper fabrics for the twenties wedding!"

"Barbarian!"

"Maybe I should have used beads that were ten cents less per dozen as well. I'm going to do the dresses for *this* wedding as I like even if we won't make much money. The velvet and satin I want to use are *very* expensive, and the client isn't wealthy. But the challenge and good public relations will make it worth my while," she told Barney. "I'll buy the fabric and do the patterns, *then* tell my partner when it's too late for him to interfere."

"Good for you, Morgana, darling." Barney patted her shoulder. "One must preserve artistic integrity!"

"Right! Besides, I'd like to enjoy my work without worrying about the cost of buttons or hooks and eyes," she continued. "Oh, Barney, I'm so tired of fighting with Nicholas. He insists on investigating every tiny purchase I make. And he has to co-sign all checks. I know he's behaving like this just to make me miserable."

"Poor darling."

140

"I've asked Charlotte to call me at my home number rather than at the office. I'm afraid the answering service will give *him* a message from her."

The answering service had been another of Nicholas Bedford's ideas. It was one more way to make sure he kept the upper hand, she thought. Morgana shook her head wryly, remembering how she had thought she would be giving Nicholas a difficult time with her revised contract. Somehow, he had managed to turn the tables on her. She had to escape his control!

Morgana didn't know what she would have done without Barney. He'd been sympathetic and understanding. He called daily, stopped by frequently, and was consistently on time. Barney's warm presence helped Morgana survive her encounters with the cold and disdainful stranger Nicholas had become.

"I appreciate your support." Morgana hugged her old friend. "If only I could buy out Nicholas . . . but it'll be years before I have the money!"

"I'd help you if I could."

Barney stared at the floor. Wanting to lighten his mood once more, Morgana jumped up to get a bulging manila envelope from the desk. She handed it to him with a chuckle. "Here's something to keep the financial wizard's eyes open a few nights."

Barney examined the package. "What is it?"

"Mr. Bedford requested full reports of past weddings to figure out profit margins," Morgana explained with a snide smile. "I gave him what he asked for. It took *days* to complete. Each report is more than twenty pages long. Every detail is there, down to the bandages I bought to patch up my fingers!"

"Petty, petty." Barney clucked. "I love it, my dear!"

"Nicholas wants these reports tomorrow, so you'll have to deliver them to his office. I've put checks to be signed in the envelope, too."

"Are deliveries part of my job description?" Barney asked.

"Didn't you read it?"

Morgana giggled, thinking of the complete job description Nicholas had drawn up for Barney. That was in addition to the expense report forms.

"Certainly, I did *not* read it. I threw out the whole packet. I've never had a job description in my life, and I don't intend to follow one now." Barney stood regally and threw a length of fabric over his sweat shirt like a cape. "I suppose I should get started if I have to reach Bedford's office by tomorrow."

Laughing at his sarcasm, Morgana accompanied him to the door.

"Bedford should stick to accounting," Barney complained. "He wants to commercialize *our* creative venture. Did he tell you he wants to offer wedding packages by mail? And he intends to produce huge weddings to serve as PR events for Fantasy Weddings so he can franchise the business." Barney's voice was rising. "One can't franchise creativity!" In another minute Morgana knew she would be audience to a full-blown and thunderous speech.

"I'm sure he's just talking," she said soothingly. "Let me handle it. Nicholas can't do anything without my agreement. I think he may be trying to irritate you."

"He's succeeded!"

"Don't worry about his grand ideas," Morgana advised, concerned she might lose Barney. The actor wasn't tied to Fantasy Weddings as she was. "If you have problems, tell *me* about them. We'll have to take care of each other."

As if he had sensed Morgana's thoughts, Barney said to assure her, "Of course, darling. I won't leave you in the lurch." Opening the door, he gave his cape one last dramatic flap. "Onward bravely! We shall ride together to victory!"

Morgana absentmindedly wandered back to her sketches, thinking about the changes Nicholas wanted to make in the business. What should she do about the personnel Nicholas wanted to hire? She had no objection to a full-time seamstress, but did they need a public relations expert? What costs would she have to cut in order to afford such a luxury? She wanted to save money but not at the expense of quality.

Nicholas was doing a good job of making her miserable. Was he resentful of the cool way she handled him? Did he still care about her?

Answers to her myriad questions eluded Morgana. Several days later she was still wondering how to handle Nicholas as she prepared coffee for their biweekly business meeting.

Nicholas made a racket as he entered. She turned to see him glower at her. Color suffused his cheekbones, and his eyes blazed. Morgana flinched, remembering how those eyes had once burned with another, softer emotion.

"Want some coffee?" she asked, pushing aside her memories. Drawing a deep breath, she squared her shoulders for the battle she was sure would ensue.

Nicholas threw a folder on the table. "I demand some explanations, Morgana. How is it you're scheduling weddings without my approval?"

Morgana's heart dropped. He found out about the Claffey wedding! "What are you talking about?" she asked, bluffing.

"This supposed client called me at my office yesterday after the answering service had given her my number. Her name was Clancey, Claffey—something on that order. Ring a bell, Morgana?"

She was going to have to think fast. Why did Charlotte have to use the office number? "Well, uh . . ."

"Don't bother denying it. Guilt is written all over your face."

Taking a dainty sip of coffee, Morgana tried to appear collected. "Charlotte Claffey asked about designing dresses for her wedding in November." She added airily, "The plans are not confirmed."

"*She* seems to think so."

"Oh, really?"

"As a matter of fact, she thinks you've completed designs for her. She called to say she'll have one fewer bridesmaid."

"Well, I planned to tell you when your responsibility as financial partner entered into our dealing. The plans are not confirmed," she insisted.

Nicholas's eyes narrowed. "Not confirmed, huh? That's good. Because I just canceled an order from Friedman's Fabrics. They called to say they could only get a limited supply of the rust-colored satin. I told them to forget it. The order was a mistake."

"What!" Morgana's mouth flew open. That material was available nowhere else. "You had no right to do that!"

"Ah-ha!" Nicholas said. "You're supposed to confer with me about materials and expenses."

"I *planned* to confer with you. I simply ordered the material first because it's so hard to find. Now you've really held things up. You have no right to interfere with the creative part of the business!"

"You gave me the right to interfere when you accepted me as a partner and carefully outlined my responsibilities," Nicholas insisted. "I've been trying to fulfill my duties—as limited as you've made them. I have the right to expect you to fulfill yours."

Morgana controlled her rapid breathing so she wouldn't fly into a rage. She must remember she had to continue working with this impossible man. Reaching for the coffee-pot, she poured herself another cup.

"More coffee?" she asked him through gritted teeth.

Nicholas looked at his full cup as if he hadn't noticed it before. Quickly he drank it all. Morgana refilled it, wishing she could add a potion to the beverage, one that would turn Nicholas into a disgusting frog . . . or back into her own true knight.

"All right," Morgana said grudgingly. "I'll send you a detailed report about this new wedding. But I'm going to reorder the material!"

Nicholas didn't object. He took a swig from his cup and announced, "Now, on to the next subject. When the hell is the barbarian wedding?"

Morgana almost spit out her coffee. "Barbarian wedding?"

"Not again," he muttered.

"There isn't any barbarian wedding."

"Don't play coy."

"Honestly. I give you my word." Was he losing his mind? "Where did you get such an outlandish idea?"

"From an outlandish person! Who else but Barney would arrive in time to interrupt a special board meeting in my office? He barged into the boardroom, wearing a horned helmet and some kind of fur wrap. I'm sure he thoroughly enjoyed the stir he caused. When I asked him to explain the meaning of his remarkable attire, he said he was preparing for the barbarian nuptials."

"I don't know anything about a barbarian wedding. I sent Barney over with the checks and reports for you."

Nicholas inspected her closely. Morgana thought he believed her.

"That doesn't alter the fact he delivered your ridiculous reports three days late." Nicholas glared at her. "Barney is irresponsible, incompetent, and inefficient."

Not wanting to hear anything bad about the only person who seemed concerned about her, Morgana avoided his eyes and angrily poured Nicholas more coffee. The steaming liquid splashed over the rim and onto his fingers.

"Ouch!"

"Have some more coffee."

"Don't avoid the issue, Morgana. You know Barney's always late. He doesn't keep regular hours. We never know *where* he is. I've tried to call him many times and reached some place called the Nomad Theater Group. There must have been twenty different people who have answered the phone, but no one knew where he was."

"Maybe we should buy him a CB," she suggested sarcastically.

"He wouldn't stay in his van."

"A beeper?"

"Quit being smart. If an employee can't be responsible, we don't need him."

"Are you saying that Barney should be fired?"

Nicholas didn't answer immediately. He pulled a yellow paper from his suit pocket and threw it on the table. *"This* is what Barney presented as a monthly expense report. He got a ticket when he double-parked in front of my office building. What do *you* think?"

Covering her smile with one hand, Morgana refilled

Nicholas's half-empty cup. "Barney is just being humorous. You don't understand him."

"I don't want to understand that kind of humor. When he finally returned my call, it was at my home, in the middle of the night!" Nicholas raised his cup to his mouth. "Whew!" he exploded, spilling brown drops of liquid on his shirtfront. "This coffee is still hot! Stop refilling it, will you?"

"Perhaps Barney should report *only* to me," she suggested. "I can handle him."

"Oh, no. Employees have to be able to work with both partners. I'm going to fire him."

"You can't fire anyone without my approval."

"Then I'm lowering his salary."

"You can't do that either."

"Then I think you should pay him out of *your* share of the profits."

"Hah!"

Abruptly Nicholas looked at his watch. "I can't stay here any longer. Here are the checks. I'll enter them in the books tomorrow. I won't comment on your reports. It'll take me awhile to decipher them."

Morgana smiled.

"As I'm sure you planned," he said on his way to the door.

"Phone before you come tomorrow," she called after him sweetly. For once he hadn't left holding the upper hand.

Why did thinking about their game of one-upmanship make her feel so sad? Morgana decided she had drunk too much coffee again as she tossed and turned throughout the night. She awoke with a start from a light doze. It was only seven in the morning, but someone was moving around downstairs. A burglar! After struggling to get out of bed, she thrust her arms into a kimono and grasped the most dangerous thing she could find, a heavy fabric weight. Carefully she sneaked down the stairway. Heart pounding, she prepared to meet the intruder as she made her way to the office.

A woman with a smooth brown pageboy and an immaculate navy suit was looking through her desk drawers. She didn't *look* like a burglar.

"What are you doing here?" Morgana asked challengingly.

The young woman jumped, turning a frightened face. Her eyes were wide behind horn-rimmed glasses. "I'm collecting the ledgers for Mr. Bedford."

Morgana instantly recognized the nasal voice.

"I'm his secretary, Ruth Hartford," the woman explained. "He gave me the keys. I'm to take the books to our office."

"You're not taking the books anywhere. They belong here."

The secretary hesitated. "But Mr. Bedford said—"

"I don't care what he said! If he wants the books, he can come and get them himself!"

"All right." Ms. Hartford acquiesced, retreating from Morgana as if she were a raging maniac. "I'll tell him."

Morgana suddenly realized she had been waving the fabric weight around like a weapon. After Ms. Hartford had left, Morgana made sure the door was locked. She was furious! Now complete strangers were invading her home and work space. She would take care of this immediately. At eight o'clock she called the locksmith and had him install new dead bolts.

148

Later that night, as she brushed her hair, she hummed. She had had a cup of cocoa and turned back the sheets. Planning to go to bed early, she felt deliciously tired.

Morgana was shocked when the doorbell rang insistently. The harsh sound made her spine jangle. Since she had made no appointments with clients, it could be only *one* person. The doorbell buzzed again and again. She padded to the front window. Looking out, she saw a familiar silver sedan parked under the streetlight.

Too bad for him, Morgana thought. He could get the new keys at their next meeting. Determined to ignore the situation, she threw her brush on an antique chest. She was going to bed.

Soon heavy pounding replaced the buzzing. Was he planning to break the door down? Morgana returned to the window and opened the sash wide. Sticking her head out, she shouted, "What do you want?"

"Morgana!" Nicholas stepped out onto the lawn. "Open the damn door!"

"Go away! You can call me tomorrow!"

"I'm going to see you tonight! Open the door, or our contract is null and void!"

"I can't hear you! Come back tomorrow!"

Attracted to a conversation that could take place only at a yelling level, several curious neighbors were looking out their windows.

Nicholas cupped his hands around his mouth. "You can hear me, Morgana! I've got to have access to the facilities!"

An elderly lady walking her tiny white dog paused on the sidewalk behind him. "Facilities?" the lady questioned. "Young man, I believe there are rest rooms in the service stations throughout this neighborhood."

"I'm not talking about rest rooms!" Nicholas shouted,

then lowered his voice when he turned to face his spectator. "Excuse me, madam," he explained politely. "This is a private conversation."

"Excuse *me,*" the woman said, but continued to stand where she was.

"Morgana!" Nicholas yelled up at her window. "We're causing a scene!" The small dog began to yap as it leaped and bounced around his feet. "Morgana, let me in!"

Sighing with resignation, Morgana tightened her kimono's sash and headed downstairs. When she opened the front door, Nicholas was cursing as he extricated his pants leg from the dog's teeth.

"Here, Fluffy!" called the elderly lady.

"Why don't you keep Fluffy on a leash?" Nicholas made the parting remark as he shouldered past Morgana.

"You couldn't have waited until tomorrow?" Morgana snapped, closing the door.

"Why should I? I was supposed to do the ledgers today. I didn't receive them since you threw my secretary out and threatened her with violence."

"I didn't threaten her," Morgana argued. "Besides, you aren't supposed to remove the books."

"And I'm not supposed to be here except at your convenience. And I'm not supposed to have the keys anymore. And I'm not to criticize your friend, Barney. What other rules have you made for me lately?"

"Rules!" Morgana sputtered. "You should be talking, Mr. Banker Bedford. I'm sick of reports and pennypinching and fighting!"

"You put me in this role," Nicholas said coldly. "Perhaps I got carried away in response to your own pettiness."

"You're blaming *me* for your terrible behavior? You're not going to control me! Let me tell you—"

"Enough!"

Morgana was silent. Nicholas looked at her intently. His expression was sad. She could hear the emotion in his voice. "This isn't working out, and you know it. Maybe you even planned it so I'd be happy to sell when you could afford to buy me out."

That touched a nerve in Morgana. But why should the truth bring with it an awful surge of guilt? After all, he'd begun their business relationship with deceit.

"What a mess!" Nicholas ran his fingers back through his hair, disheveling it. "I had hoped this second business would give me some creative satisfaction, something different from my normal work. You ruined it for me by insisting on that stupid contract."

Morgana swallowed the lump in her throat. Nicholas had ruined much more for her than work satisfaction. Quickly she blinked back her tears.

"You've been horrible to me!" she cried.

"You've been pretty hostile yourself. The major reason I bought into this business was that I cared about you. I went along with the damn contract thinking we could work things out when you calmed down. What has happened here? You've done your best to make us enemies."

Nicholas's statement penetrated Morgana's overwhelming emotions. He cared? After all they'd been through, could she believe him? Her pain made her accuse him. "Me? I made us enemies? You're the one who drew up contracts behind my back."

Nicholas's eyes glistened as he drew a ragged breath. "You can never forget that, can you? Or try to understand? I went about it in the wrong way, and you've never let me explain." He turned to walk away. "I give up. I may as well go home. You can do as you like about the keys."

Morgana's lips quivered as she held herself in check.

Nicholas stood in the open doorway. He touched her cheek tenderly, the gesture so unexpected she didn't move away. "You're beautiful with your hair all loose around your face, Morgana. This is the way I like to remember you. I made a big mistake mixing business with romance."

After the door had closed, she burst into tears.

CHAPTER TEN

Although Morgana didn't see Nicholas during the remainder of the week, he was seldom far from her thoughts. Over and over she replayed his last words to her. She wanted to believe them or at least the part where he said his interest in *her* was the primary reason he'd bought into Fantasy Weddings.

Had he been serious? And had he been correct when he accused her of ruining any pleasure he might get from the business? Truthful with herself, Morgana thought about the situation long and hard and came up with some unsettling answers.

Before Nicholas planned to buy out her sister in secret, Morgana had believed he was an honest man, sincere by nature, if not open emotionally. Had she been mistaken—or had he had good intentions in making the deal with Blanche? Perhaps her judgment of him had been too harsh, her anger too protracted. After all, she had made peace with her sister.

Shouldn't she forgive Nicholas as well?

Barney had said something to that effect only the day before. She'd sent him to Nicholas's office with the new set of keys. Returning in an oddly pensive mood, he'd muttered that one couldn't hold a grudge forever. . . . Had Nicholas and Barney reconciled?

Evasive under her questioning, Barney did impart an invitation from Nicholas. He wanted her to join him at Pablo's Tacos to have dinner with his first prospective clients this evening.

On her way there now Morgana wondered how to approach a rational discussion of their relationship—both business and personal. She'd taken a cab into the city, knowing Nicholas would have to drive her home. If only they both could control their tempers.

Morgana wistfully thought of the last time she'd been in his car, close to him, one hand on his thigh. It had been the stormy night of Mariette's wedding. She'd felt such love and such apprehension. How ironic that she'd feared the wrong question. Or had she? What had been the rest of Nicholas's proposal? She had never let him finish his explanation. Perhaps he *had* wanted to ask her to marry him. . . .

The questions rolled around in her mind until the cab pulled over to the corner nearest Pablo's Tacos. She filed her thoughts away, ready to be called up later, when Nicholas took her home.

Pablo's was a difficult place to miss. Announced by a swinging neon sign, the restaurant was housed in a one-story building, its brick front painted a brilliant turquoise. Huge handprinted signs advertising specials were taped in the windows.

"Enchilada plate, four twenty-five," Morgana read out loud.

What a strange place to meet, Morgana decided on entering the restaurant. Pablo's Tacos was not her partner's style. The huge room had a hand-carved bar and clusters of small tables covered with plastic cloths in bright colors. Piñatas and plants hung from the ceiling, and colorful paintings with velvet backgrounds decorated the walls.

Nicholas sat beneath a vibrant rendition of an Aztec saving a scantily clad maiden. Morgana smothered a grin as she made her way to the table where he was entertaining a middle-aged couple.

The two men stood. When Nicholas made the introductions, his smile actually seemed genuine. "Morgana Lawrence, this is Mrs. Cooke and Mr. Perez."

"How do you do?" Morgana said, shaking hands with them.

"Oh, I'm so excited!" the cheery little woman exclaimed. "You have such a marvelous reputation for organizing unique weddings. I have to admit my first was a tad dull, my dear," Mrs. Cooke confided, patting Morgana's arm, her tiny hand loaded down with a gigantic diamond engagement ring. "Marcos and I want to make a big splash no one will ever forget!"

Morgana stared, fascinated by the bride-to-be. Her friendly smile certainly outshone her haphazard graying hair and the dullness of her plain dark dress. "We do our best to give our clients their dream wedding," she said faintly.

"Money is no object. My late husband owned the Cooke hardware chain, you know. He had other investments, including a share of Pablo's Tacos. That's how I met Marcos. He's one of Pablo's younger brothers." She rattled on. "They own a chain now. Marcos oversees several, and I plan to help." The bride threw her stocky, mustached groom a coquettish kiss. "We'll mix love and business. Isn't it romantic?"

Morgana glanced at her own partner, wishing their situation could be so romantic. The other man caught her attention with his toast.

"To you, *querida*." Raising his glass to his fiancée,

155

Marcos smiled broadly, his white teeth flashing against his tanned skin.

"Have a margarita, Morgana," Nicholas said, pouring her a glass from a large pitcher.

"Yes, do," Mrs. Cooke urged. "I'd like to toast the beginning of a wonderful association!"

Their fingers touched as Nicholas handed Morgana her drink. "To new beginnings," he said, raising an eyebrow.

How long had it been since Morgana had received that look? It made her heart trip alarmingly. She squirmed in her chair, unwilling to give in so easily to the thrill creeping through her. In spite of herself, Morgana devoured Nicholas with her eyes. Dressed in a black knit pullover and slacks, he could be a Spanish nobleman. The severity of his clothes complemented his well-defined features and accented the silver in his hair.

Determined to distract herself from such dangerous thoughts—for they hadn't settled anything between them, had they?—Morgana turned to their client. "Well, Mrs. Cooke, why don't we begin discussing your wedding plans?"

"The name's Janet, dear. Formality makes me uncomfortable," the bride-to-be insisted as a huge plate of nachos arrived. "I want a spectacular wedding, very romantic," she said between bites of crisp tortilla smothered with guacamole, refried beans, cheese, and sour cream. "Naturally it *must* have a Latin flavor. Marcos's heritage is *so* exciting." Janet gave her groom-to-be a searing glance, which he returned immediately.

Touched by the adoration she witnessed in their silent exchange, Morgana concentrated on her margarita so she wouldn't have to turn to Nicholas.

"Drink up," he urged. "There's plenty more."

From his knowing inflection Morgana decided he could

read her mind. "I'd better take it easy. This is pretty potent stuff," she mumbled.

"If you're not careful, you might let go," Nicholas said, gravely agreeing. "You might even see things with a different perspective."

A quick glance at him made Morgana flush. There was a familiar light in those silver gray eyes she was finding difficult to ignore.

Morgana forced her attention back to her clients. "Did you have anything specific in mind?"

"A beautiful long table," Marcos chimed in enthusiastically. "In the center a *magnífico* cake with many columns. Then, on each side, a smaller cake with the bridges to connect," he explained, drawing the whole thing in the air with his hands while Morgana watched in awe. "The frostings, they must be in bright colors. And we want pretty birds and flowers. Many, many birds and flowers. My brother Julio had one just so. No worry, my cousin Hector owns a bakery. He can make it!"

It was more than the little man had said since she arrived. Visualizing the towering creation he'd described, Morgana realized it would be bigger than the groom himself. It was overwhelming, just as the prospective clients were becoming.

Cautiously she asked, "Won't it be a little large?"

"Oh, no," Janet said assuringly. "Marcos has hundreds of relatives. And I plan to invite more than a hundred guests myself. Perhaps we should have other desserts, too. You know, flan and sweet breads and something very chocolate. We wouldn't want anyone to be disappointed," she added. "Of course, we want the traditional foods. Tacos, enchiladas, flautas, refried beans. But equally important is the setting. It must be very gay," Janet insisted with a dramatic

157

flourish that reminded Morgana of Barney. "Fountains and flowers all over. And how about flying doves?"

"And Mexican flags!" suggested Marcos. "And many piñatas *para los niños.* My family is blessed with children."

"Certainly, *querido.*" Janet caressed her man with her eyes.

Morgana looked questioningly at Nicholas. His face was a blank, but his Adam's apple bobbed as he swallowed hard.

"O-o-oh, and we can have mariachis, dressed in those wonderful suits with the silver buttons down the legs, playing guitars and trumpets for the ceremony," Janet said with enthusiasm. "And flamenco dancers! They'd be great at the reception!"

So this was her partner's idea of an elaborate wedding that would serve as a PR event! The entire affair sounded like an exercise in questionable taste. Suspiciously she glanced at Nicholas. He was staring at the floor, holding a napkin over his mouth. His shoulders were shaking. Was this his idea of a joke? When he looked up at her, his expression bore a mixture of amusement and pained bewilderment. It was no joke.

"I can't wait until you design my gown, Morgana," Janet continued. "I envision a tight-fitting flamenco dress with tiers of white lace and gold lamé. And Marcos can be dressed as a matador. We'll make a dramatic entrance, especially if you choreograph some steps so we could dance down the aisle."

Janet watched her expectantly, and Morgana downed another margarita. She'd be diplomatic, but if the couple didn't approve of her suggestions, she would refuse the wedding. The event they described wouldn't enhance Fantasy Weddings' reputation.

"If you want the dramatic," Morgana said carefully,

158

"then I'd suggest something more understated. Often simplicity is the most effective approach."

Nicholas made a strangled sound, and Morgana stared at him, horrified. How could he insult prospective clients?

But immediately Janet's rich laughter released Nicholas's inhibitions. He laughed openly. Marcos chortled, fingering his full mustache. The sound was infectious, sweeping Morgana into a like mood. If this was a joke after all, it was a good one. Morgana laughed, wondering if Janet and Marcos were friends of Barney's. If not, the actor would insist on meeting them!

"More margaritas!" Marcos called to a waitress.

"I guess we got a little carried away," Janet admitted, still giggling. "It's just that this wedding is so important to us. We want to remember it always," she said softly, placing her hand in that of her future husband. He covered it with his other hand and patted her reassuringly. "I trust your judgment, Morgana. What would you suggest?"

So they *were* real clients. Morgana respected the fact that they could laugh at their grandiose suggestions.

"You have some good ideas," she told Janet.

"And we can adapt them to give you a dream wedding you'll never forget," Nicholas added.

"Wonderful. You know how it is when you're in love." Janet sighed. "Even the most extreme fantasies seem perfectly logical."

"Yes, it's easy to get carried away," Morgana said in agreement, gazing at Nicholas. His eyes beckoned to her, making Morgana anxious to finish the meeting and take advantage of the ride home.

Turning back to the clients, she pulled out her notebook and pen and did a rough sketch. "I can make you a version of the traditional Mexican wedding dress. Like this. And fresh flowers in your hair would be beautiful, don't you think?"

Janet approved. Nicholas leaned over the table for a closer look, resting his knee against Morgana's. Warmth spread up her thigh, distracting her, but she didn't move away.

"Why not have the mariachis at the reception?" Nicholas suggested. "A single guitar at the ceremony would give it a very classy touch."

"Perfect!" Janet told him.

"I'd suggest miniature Mexican specialties as appetizers and paella for the main course," Morgana told them.

"Morgana, you are a gem!"

"We could set up a punch table and spike fresh fruit juices with tequila. And fresh flowers could be strewn on the table itself," Nicholas added. "It'll remind everyone of a Mexican resort."

"I'd love that. We're going to Acapulco for our honeymoon."

"But we must have the cake," Marcos insisted. "I cannot disappoint Hector."

"All right." Morgana laughed. "The cake stays."

As they ate and talked, Morgana decided she liked Janet Cooke. She was open and honest, with no presumptions about herself.

"Are you and Nicholas going together?" Janet asked frankly. "You seem so perfect for each other. And your work is *so* romantic!" She sighed. "I'd be surprised if it *didn't* affect you."

Morgana sidestepped a direct answer. "The work definitely influences my way of thinking." How else had Nicholas Bedford been turned into a Spanish nobleman?

160

"Had any interesting ideas lately?" Nicholas asked her with an innocent expression.

"They may come to me," she answered, thinking of the ride home.

"Tell me when. I wouldn't want to miss anything."

His intense gaze brought back a tidal wave of repressed emotions and memories of physical pleasure. She remembered his kisses, the texture of his skin against hers. . . .

Under the table Nicholas caught one of her hands and pressed it gently, his long fingers massaging her palm. Every capillary pounded with excitement, telegraphing the message through her veins.

The dinner hour was long over when the two couples decided to leave. They had a deal. Nicholas would draw up a contract immediately, and Morgana would contact Janet in a few weeks.

Walking to the car hand in hand with Nicholas, Morgana halfheartedly admonished herself to be careful. She wasn't about to jump back into a physical relationship before they'd settled things between them. There were still issues to discuss, weren't there?

"You handled the situation beautifully," Nicholas told her. "I admire your tact. I don't know what I would have done alone. I had no idea they'd want an outlandish wedding. Your suggestions were perfect," he said, starting the car and heading it toward home.

"You made a few good suggestions yourself."

"Perhaps, but you're the creative genius of Fantasy Weddings."

"I have the most experience," she admitted. "I've been thinking about what you said last week. How you wanted to become part of a more creative business? I guess I did spoil that for you when I demanded the revised contract." She

161

swallowed. "Perhaps I was unfair. I haven't any objection to your sharing some of the creative decision making if you want."

"I'd like to share things with you," Nicholas admitted. Morgana was sure the business was not the only thing he was referring to. "And I'm sorry I got carried away by my resentment and gave you a difficult time." Nicholas laid his arm over the back of the seat. "I was so disappointed with the situation. When I was young, I had some artistic ability. I took drawing and design classes in college. Then my stepfather died, and I was responsible for Sondra and Mari. I had to be practical, so I went for an M.B.A. I guess I never realized how frustrated I've been until I met you."

"Well, you won't have to be frustrated anymore."

"Oh? I'd like to discuss that more fully. Why don't you move closer?" Nicholas suggested, his voice husky.

Morgana's resolve to be cautious was slowly disintegrating, yet she couldn't abandon it altogether. She slid a few inches closer and breathed deeply of his scent—cologne mingling with his own masculine essence. She stared ahead at the road.

"Nicholas, when did you decide to try to talk things out with me?" she asked.

"When Barney told me you were in love with me."

"What!" She'd kill Barney! "Why did . . . uh, how . . ."

"Calm down," Nicholas said. "I'll explain. When you sent Barney with the keys, I figured it was as good a time as any to get things straight with him. He was making me crazy, and you wouldn't let me fire him, so the only thing left was to talk to him."

"Why would he tell you . . . what he told you?" Morgana demanded, her heart pounding.

"I requested he explain his behavior. He was doing all those crazy things out of loyalty to you." He chuckled. "He was terribly indignant that I'd hurt you so badly. Until then I was seeing only my side of the story. I couldn't believe you wouldn't listen to me, and the contract really set me off. If I'd kept cool, we might have been able to straighten this out sooner," he admitted. "Anyway, Barney set me straight about several things, the most important of which was how you feel about me."

Knowing that was her cue, Morgana couldn't bring herself to confirm the truth: She was still in love with Nicholas Bedford, for better or for worse.

He didn't seem to expect an answer, for Nicholas said nothing more, yet he rested his hand on her thigh. Her flesh burned there, the heat a welcome one.

How had she done without Nicholas for so long? she wondered. He'd been so close yet so distant.

Turning to him, Morgana inspected his profile and giggled softly as she remembered her imaginings in the restaurant.

"What was that for?"

"Oh, I was just thinking of how you remind me of a regal Spanish nobleman in your black clothes."

"I thought I was your knight."

"That was before. Now you're my mysterious caballero."

"And you're my wild-haired Spanish gypsy," Nicholas whispered, joining her fantasy. He slipped his hand from her thigh and found her hand, which he brought to his lips without taking his eyes from the road. His mouth seared her with his desire.

Silently Morgana blessed him with a love spell, one to make him want her desperately—as desperately as she wanted him. Luckily they were almost home.

163

When they pulled up in front of her building, Nicholas left the engine running and turned to her. His eyes told her the spell was working. Obviously he was waiting for an invitation.

"Would you like to come inside, señor?"

The engine was off and the keys were in his hand almost before she had finished her question.

A golden haze of anticipation enveloping her, Morgana led the way into her apartment. Yet once inside she became more awkward with Nicholas than she'd ever been.

Nervously she turned on one light after another while he stood in her doorway, watching the unnecessary action with passion-filled eyes. Then, just as deliberately, he followed her trail, flicking off each light. One after another, until he'd caught up with her and pinned her against the antique breakfront. Moonlight filtered through the windows, bathing the room—and Nicholas—with a seductive silver glow. His familiar male scent enticed her anew.

Ever so slowly his lips touched her forehead; his tongue traced her widow's peak and followed the line of her hair down to one ear. At the same time Morgana shivered, her insides melted.

"I want you with music, my wild-haired gypsy," he whispered, the sound so seductive it made her heart race.

Something caught in her throat—an overwhelming emotion denying her speech. She nodded in assent.

Nicholas turned on the radio and tuned in a Spanish station. Soft Latin music evoked sensual images for Morgana, ones she hoped he would make real before the sun rose.

"Come, señorita," Nicholas softly commanded, opening his arms to her. "Dance with me."

Morgana stepped into his arms, reentering the magical world she had missed so fiercely. As their bodies swayed to a slow, provocative rumba rhythm, Nicholas nuzzled her brow and ran his fingers along the back of her neck. The atmosphere around them grew heavy with repressed passion, a mixture of pain and sweetness reflecting its intensity.

Strangely frightened by the emotions he rekindled in her so easily, Morgana attempted to lighten the atmosphere with frivolous conversation. "Ah, señor, you are a wonderful dancer."

"Only with you, my Spanish gypsy. You inspire me with your supple body and your graceful movements to the music."

"Perhaps I will dance for you then, señor. I have the most wonderful Spanish dress with tiers and tiers of taffeta ruffles. Give me but a moment—"

"Don't bother. It would be a waste of time."

"But why?"

"I'd just have to tear it off you."

His words evoked powerful images, ones to which Morgana willingly succumbed. Why should she fight them when she did not want to?

Resting her head against his, Morgana indulged herself, weaving an irreversible spell around them both. She would always be his fantasy, she vowed. And he would be hers.

Lovers throughout eternity. What a beautiful thought!

She had danced for him, and he was well pleased, this Spanish nobleman of hers. And now he would return the pleasure. His warm breath stirred the hair at her temple. Hot hands roamed her body, intensifying emotion and sensation. Whirling for him one last time, she felt her clothing being stripped from her body.

A light kiss on the lips—oh, so unsatisfying, for it was over too quickly—and her Spanish conqueror was off, exploring new territories.

"Ah, a treasure," he whispered, finding a breast to nuzzle.

Morgana wrapped her hands around his head, pressing Nicholas closer to nurture her. Not content to remain there long either, he pressed on to new discoveries.

"But my reward for the dance . . ." she protested.

". . . is yet to come," he finished.

His mouth left a burning trail along her stomach. He knelt, slipping his hands around her buttocks, holding her tight to him. Running his lips along her hipbone, Nicholas used his hands to knead her until every fiber of her body felt on fire. It was when she moaned that he dipped his head lower, nipping the inside of her thighs to make them part.

Liquid sensation shot through her lower body, and his lips moved to meet it. Nicholas loved her until her knees buckled.

"Perhaps the bed?" she whispered hoarsely, but Morgana suddenly realized she was on the floor, the smooth oak cool under her back.

And the loving hadn't stopped but had intensified.

Morgana arched to his mouth, unable to do more than delight in her reward. His tongue coaxed forth every bud of desire stored in her, while his hands roamed upward until they reached her breasts. If possible, her nipples grew larger with each exquisite stroke of his fingers.

"Nicholas," she whispered, the word electric with excitement.

His answer was a moan, but although she tried to force his head upward to meet her waiting mouth, he wouldn't leave his task. Morgana writhed in response as the tension rose within her. The music filtering through the room was an erotic piece, its tempo building, as did hers. Behind Morgana's closed eyelids, colorful flowers bloomed, their exotic fragrance filling her senses.

When the inner explosion came, it was short but intense, relieving all the frustration built up during their separation. Morgana was slicked with sweat, and Nicholas slipped up to kiss her.

"An appropriate reward, I hope?" he murmured before kissing her again.

"Ah, but, señor, you have only teased my passions," she said breathlessly. "I hope you do not expect to get off so lightly."

"Command me," Nicholas whispered. "No reward is too great for your sweetness, my gypsy."

"I desire the removal of your clothes."

It was done in seconds, and Morgana commanded Nicholas to lie still while she explored his body as he had hers. She would know the taste of every inch of his flesh, she thought, trailing her lips across his stomach and over his thighs. Excitement burst within her as she dared to run her mouth down the length of him, but before she could do more, he proved to be an impatient lover.

As her tongue matched the softness of his, he threw her over with a groan and kissed her deeply. His own tongue entered her forcefully, demanding a like response. Morgana gave it willingly, tangling her fingers in his hair once more, holding on to him with the strength of her passion.

Somehow, Nicholas managed to lift them both from the floor without breaking his embrace. His kiss deepened as he whirled her to the bed and fell to the softness locked in her embrace.

"Love me, Nicholas," she commanded.

Pressing her deep into the quilted mattress, Nicholas entered her gently, drawing out the pleasure. Then he began an erotic dance, the movement enticing her back into their other world.

167

Morgana slipped her hands down the length of his body, memorizing every change of texture with her fingertips. When her hands reached his buttocks, she left them there, mesmerized by the feel of rippling muscles as he moved within her.

Nicholas pressed a fleeting kiss to her lips before moving lower. After trailing his lips down the column of her throat, he pressed on to her soft breasts below. Little bites stirred her, making Morgana dig her nails into his buttocks.

"Querida," he whispered, before taking a nipple into his mouth, testing its hardness with his teeth.

"M-m-m. Oh, yes, my caballero, take the treasure. The reward is to be shared," she teased, while reality faded completely.

Their erotic dance built slowly, neither seeming to want it to end. Their movement matched the music, the pace changing with each piece. Morgana didn't know how Nicholas held out so long, their lovemaking seeming to last a sweet eternity.

When the end came for him, he cried out, the sound triggering Morgana's own release. They floated down together, and without moving from his embrace, Morgana felt herself drifting into a peaceful oblivion.

She woke sometime later, in the quiet morning hours. The light of dawn cast an early-morning glow over the form of her sleeping partner.

Partner. It sounded so right, she thought, studying his peaceful features. Right in every way. Clearheaded about many things at last, Morgana admitted something to herself: Her overreaction to his and Blanche's deal had been due only in part to the hurt she'd felt in being surprised. Nicholas *had* planned to ask her to marry him; she was sure of it now. But she'd never let him explain that part of his proposal because she'd been terrified of it. She hadn't been ready, and she'd thought it would hang between them, ruining their relationship.

So, Morgana thought wryly, she'd done her best to ruin it instead. Of course, Nicholas hadn't been innocent himself.

But now everything was different. She knew exactly how important Nicholas was to her. It was more than love she felt. He was a part of her. When he walked out of her private life, the magic had gone with him. Her imagination had failed her, leaving her without the ability to fantasize, and it had returned only last night.

It was a kind of sign, Morgana thought, an indication they were meant for each other. If Nicholas asked her to marry him now, she was ready to make the commitment. She was sure he would ask, for he knew she loved him just as he loved her. Morgana frowned as she realized he'd never told her so. But he'd changed his attitude after talking to Barney, so it must mean . . .

"Frowning, my wild-haired gypsy?"

"Nicholas, you're awake!" How long had he been watching her while she was lost in her thoughts?

"I know exactly how to put a smile on your beautiful face," he said, slipping his hands around her breasts and rubbing both nipples with his thumbs.

"Yes, I believe you do," Morgana said breathlessly. "Why don't you show me?"

He did.

"M-m-m, the scent is driving me wild," Nicholas murmured into Morgana's neck while fondling her breasts through the sweater.

"Me or the food?" she demanded. His *hands* were driving her wild! "Now stop that or I'll ruin the omelet."

169

Morgana was standing in front of the stove, preparing breakfast as best she could under the circumstances.

"I thought you liked that!" he pouted, allowing his hands to slip lower, caressing her even more intimately.

"Nicholas!" she squealed. "I thought you wanted to eat."

"M-m-huh."

"Well, why don't you get the plates out and set the table while I finish here? And get the orange juice and start the toast."

"Spoilsport."

One last kiss on her neck, and Nicholas moved to the refrigerator. He hummed a cheerful tune.

After stirring the onions and mushrooms and chunks of sausage, Morgana added the beaten eggs and a touch of hot sauce. Making breakfast with Nicholas gave her a special feeling, allaying the light case of nerves that had struck her upon rising. Would he ask her today? she wondered again.

Nicholas had made love to her so beautifully this morning! Of course, he loved her, but she'd have to be patient. After all the arguments they'd had in the last several weeks, he might need some time before asking her to make a commitment.

Morgana felt a light nibbling on her neck.

"You again?"

"Expecting someone else?"

"Well . . . ouch! You beast!" Morgana said, rubbing her bottom where he'd whacked her.

"Shall I kiss it and make it better?"

"Not if you want breakfast," she warned.

"I'd like to say you're all the breakfast I need, but my stomach would disagree." Nicholas slipped his arms around her waist. "You know, this feels so natural and right."

"What does?" she asked, turning in his arms to face him.

170

It was going to be *now*, she realized, her heart thudding. Nicholas was going to ask her to marry him, and he was uncertain of how she would react. Caution shadowed his eyes.

"Being together like this. I mean, working out a partnership can be a difficult business. But I think I've finally found a way to solve our problems." He stroked her body seductively.

Why was he talking about business at a time like this? she wondered. And how did he think he could solve their problems? Using sex? Morgana was determined she wouldn't jump to conclusions. She tried to keep her voice light but pulled away slightly.

"Can you be more specific?"

"Well, you know. Waking up in each other's arms. Making breakfast together . . ."

Morgana remembered his empty threat about making her pay rent on the apartment or allowing him to share. Maybe it hadn't been so empty.

"You wouldn't be thinking about demanding your rights as co-owner of the building, would you?" She aimed a suspicious look at him.

"Uh, of course not." He suddenly went tense. "I mean, not exactly."

"What exactly then?"

"I didn't mean I'd have to live here, although it is more convenient to work for both of us. But the town house is much larger."

Morgana stiffened. "You mean, you want to *live together*?"

Nicholas's reaction was a grim-lipped response. "That *is* an option."

171

"I don't believe it!" She pushed by him and stalked into the living area.

Disappointment overwhelmed her. Nicholas didn't want to marry her after all. Did he even love her? Doubts returned. Miles had demanded they live together in spite of her reservations. Then, gradually, he had taken control of every aspect of her life, both personal and professional, using their physical relationship to smooth over any difficulties. She'd been too naïve to realize what was happening until it was too late. She'd been blinded by love and Miles's considerable charm then. And now? Morgana didn't know what to think.

"Morgana, I don't like what's happening here," Nicholas said as he followed her into the living area.

"You don't like it? How do you think I feel? You're making a business out of our relationship, Nicholas. Should that please me? Do you care about me, Nicholas, or do you think you can control me by making me happy in bed?"

"Where did you get *this* ridiculous idea?"

"What else am I supposed to think when you talk about partnerships and solutions to problems and living together and options all in one breath?"

"You're imagining all this, Morgana." Nicholas paced the room, but he stayed far from her. "You let these fantasies of yours get away with you. Either you're paranoid or all that creativity has warped your mind!"

"I suppose you have an explanation—"

"I'm sick of explanations," Nicholas told her. "And I'm sick of that damn artistic temperament of yours!"

"Well, you don't have to put up with it, do you?"

"No, I sure as hell don't." Grabbing his jacket, Nicholas stalked to the door. "I want my woman to trust me."

"Where are you going?"

172

"Anywhere to get some peace."

Morgana stared at the doorway long after he had departed, anger, disappointment, and uncertainty all warring within her. Had she been unfair to him? Had Miles colored her view of men so badly that she judged Nicholas's every word and action with suspicion even when there was no reason?

A strong odor emanating from the kitchen area finally caught her attention. Her eyes followed her nose and rested on a thick haze of smoke.

"My omelet!" she yelped, running to the stove.

The frying pan was ruined along with her breakfast. Morgana threw it away, wishing she could rid herself of her heartache and regret as easily.

CHAPTER ELEVEN

"Jack and Iris Simmons," Morgana read. "Who are *they?*" She anxiously stared at the cocktail napkins in her hand. Her clients were Ralph and Kim Fargate-Johnson. "Didn't you check the order when it arrived from the printer?" she demanded.

"I thought *you* did," Barney answered, pushing back his worn slouch hat. A moth-eaten raccoon coat and baggy pants completed his twenties outfit.

"What are we going to do?"

"Don't run amok, Morgana darling. I'm sure we can requisition some plain napkins from the bar."

"Check. *Please!*"

Everything else seemed to be going smoothly, Morgana noted with relief. The caterers were unboxing the hors d'oeuvres and setting them on platters. One of the bartenders was mixing the gin-spiked punch with an oar that had graced the wall above old photos of college sculling teams. It made an odd ladle, but no more so than the punch bowl— a claw-footed bathtub she'd had refinished and sterilized.

The "bathtub gin" would add to the speakeasy atmosphere provided by the Hide-Away Bar. Located in the basement of a turn-of-the-century building in Lincoln Park West, the former speakeasy had been a favorite haunt of Al Capone and his gang. Some of the original fixtures and stuffed leather booths remained. And the thick metal door with the sliding peephole was a vivid reminder of the twenties.

Morgana was pleased she finally had an opportunity to wear her grandmother's legacy to her: a pale pink beaded tunic over a flesh-colored chiffon dress. A beaded headband with an ostrich feather held her smoothly rolled tresses in place.

"Crisis resolved," Barney boomed happily. "The caterers want to know where we've stashed the cake. They're ready to set it up."

"The cake? My God, it hasn't arrived!" Morgana was horrified. "I can't believe *another* thing's gone wrong."

"Perhaps we need Bedford to keep track of the little details," Barney intoned.

"You're beginning to sound like a broken record."

"If you weren't so stubborn, he'd be here."

"Barney!" Only last week he'd been creating ways to torture Nicholas, and all out of loyalty to her. But then Barney did have a point. She'd come to the same conclusion. Morgana sighed. "You're right. I overreacted. Our relationship happened so fast it overwhelmed me. I just wasn't ready for a love relationship so soon. No doubt Nicholas Bedford has had enough of me to last him a lifetime."

What a fool she'd been, Morgana thought. Maybe living together *was* a natural step toward finalizing their relationship. However, she'd tried that route once—with Miles— and she still retained unpleasant memories of the experience. Perhaps she *could* have made an effort to understand Nicholas's cautious stand, however. But then Nicholas could have stayed and tried to convince her, she decided, working up some comforting anger. He needn't have walked out on her!

"Morgana, darling, Nicholas loves you."

Remembering that Barney had told Nicholas the same of *her,* Morgana blurted, "You're good at interpreting people's feelings."

"I utter nothing less than the truth."

"How do you know?"

"Simple. I asked the man what his intentions were. I demanded to know if he dared trifle with your affections."

"You didn't!" In spite of herself, Morgana laughed. "What did he say?"

"That his intentions were quite serious, my dear. Now don't you think we'd better find out about the cake?"

"The cake!" Morgana looked around wildly. "Where's the phone?"

Just then one of the flappers stalked by, followed by the bandleader. They were heading for the kitchen.

"Get away from me, George. I don't want to discuss it!"

"Vivian, will you listen to reason. I did *not* make a pass at Trixie. It was an accident!"

Morgana and Barney stared at each other. Not another problem! Well, she didn't have time for it. She had to track down the fugitive cake. Now, if only she could find the phone.

"Barney, there's got to be a phone around here somewhere!"

"I'll ask the bartender," he told her with extraordinary calm.

Morgana could hear raised voices from the direction of the kitchen, followed by a loud crash and the tinkling of broken glass. Would there *be* a band? she wondered.

"We looked right at it," Barney said a few seconds later and pointed. An antique-looking phone with separate receiver and speaker rested on a low table.

Moving to it, Morgana said, "I would have sworn it was a

prop." On closer inspection she noticed the coin box on the wall.

"The bartender assures me it's functional with the correct inducement."

Barney handed her two dimes.

Morgana searched under the table and under an adjoining stool, then turned upon hearing the metal door creak open. Realizing the first guests had arrived, Morgana grew frantic. "There's no phone book!"

"There are dozens of eager employees of the telephone company *breathlessly* awaiting your cry for help."

"Directory assistance!"

Calming herself, Morgana obtained the bakery's number and dialed it.

"Carter's Cakery."

"This is Morgana Lawrence. I'm calling to find out what is delaying the cake for the—"

"You'll have to talk to Mr. Carter," the male voice told her. "Hold, please."

Morgana sighed in frustration and eyed a couple who entered arm in arm.

"Ah, excuse me, but are you in charge?" One of the guests questioned them.

"Yes. Can we help you?"

"Ah, there seems to be a slight leak in the bathtub."

A stream of pink liquid shot from the side of the tub, creating a pool on the floor.

"On to the rescue!" Barney dramatically strode to the oversize punch bowl and stuck his finger in the hole. "I'll shore up at this end until reinforcements arrive."

"Ah, what a mess, huh?" The man clucked unsympathetically before wandering away.

"Carter here. You callin' about the cake?"

"Yes. For the Fargate-Johnson wedding," she told the baker.

"Should've gone out an hour ago. Hang on. I gotta talk to the driver."

"Don't tell me someone hijacked it!" Morgana muttered, but the owner had already put her on hold.

Morgana's position—crouched on the low stool—put her eyes at waist level with the people passing by. They were becoming numerous. A pair of floppy tweed knee pants paused before her. She noted a pair of bright pink socks accented by white buckskin shoes.

"Like my outfit?"

The familiar voice made her heart thud erratically and jerked her straight. Morgana allowed her eyes to travel upward, past the tweed jacket that matched his pants. He smiled down at her from beneath a ridiculous pink knit hat.

Morgana remained frozen, the receiver at her ear. She'd had no inkling Nicholas would make an appearance. And what an appearance! If she weren't so nervous, she'd be amused.

"This is an authentic twenties golfing suit—of a sort," he explained. "I had the choice of renting it or a gangster costume. I decided pink would be a little more frivolous than funereal black."

"Why are you here?" Butterflies flitted through her stomach, but Morgana tried to contain her excitement.

"I'm here to represent Fantasy Weddings, Morgana, the same as you are. What can I do?"

Barney's shout interrupted them. "Bedford! Over here!" Next to the tub of punch, one finger stuck into its side, Barney frantically gestured to Nicholas.

Morgana noted the suit was a size too large. As Nicholas made his way to Barney, it flopped around him comically.

178

More guests, including a family with several small, noisy children, arrived then. Holding tight to the receiver, Morgana strained to watch Nicholas and Barney hassle with the bathtub. Somehow, they had switched places. It was Nicholas who held back the flood now.

"We need a stopper or something gummy," she heard him say.

"Stay here," commanded Barney.

Morgana watched him stalk a small boy. Cornering the youngster, Barney waved some dollar bills before his face. The boy grinned, grabbed the money, and started to run away. But Barney was faster. Small arms flailed as the actor caught him, and clamping one hand over the small mouth, he turned the child upside down.

"Barney!" cried Morgana, outraged. "*What* are you doing?" she demanded, rising.

A man blocked her view. "Are you using the phone?"

"Huh?" Morgana looked at him reluctantly. "Yes! I'm on hold."

"Will you be long?"

"I don't know!" Morgana was exasperated. "Barney!"

The guest moved away, and she saw the actor sauntering toward Nicholas, blowing a huge pink bubble. The child was nowhere to be seen. At least he was out of danger, Morgana thought.

"Carter's Cakery," a female voice said. "May I help you?"

"Someone *is* helping me!" a frustrated Morgana told her.

"Oh. Okay."

The line went blank.

Morgana groaned. Her palms went damp, and her stomach grew queasy when she glanced at her watch. The bride and groom would arrive at any time!

179

"The leak is mended," Nicholas said, leaning over her. "Barney got bubble gum from somewhere."

"I wish everything else were mended."

"Well, so do I, but you really make it difficult."

"I *mean,* the cake. It hasn't arrived yet. I'm trying to find it!"

"Pardon me," he remarked huffily.

Suddenly the kitchen doors banged open. George and Vivian emerged, struggling. An interested murmur went up among the guests.

"You're going to fulfill your contract!" George whispered forcefully, holding on to the flapper's arm.

"I'm not working with you!" Vivian snarled as she pounded the bandleader with her small beaded bag. "Get yourself another girl friend!"

"This is a job!" George insisted. "We'll settle *our* problems later!"

The fighting couple drew near the refreshment table when Morgana rose. "I'll take care of it," Nicholas told her, pushing her down again. His warm fingers electrified her shoulder. "I think I know how they feel."

Nicholas intercepted the couple and placed an arm around each battling opponent. As they approached the small stage at the rear of the bar, Vivian tossed her head and aimed more heated words at her boyfriend, but she mounted the stage willingly. The band began to warm up.

Returning to Morgana, Nicholas grinned smugly. "Problem solved."

"What did you say to them?"

"I suggested they start thinking rationally, even though it's difficult to do so working with the person you love."

"Tell me about it," she muttered.

"Is that the voice of experience speaking?"

"What do you mean?"

"Are *you* working with the person you love? You've never told me."

"Yes, I have!" Morgana insisted. Then, thinking about it, she realized it was Barney who'd told him. "Well, you knew I did."

"It's not the same as hearing you say it."

"Why should I? You've never said it to me."

"You've never given me the chance."

"You've had plenty of chances to say a lot of things!"

"Let's not get into another ridiculous argument. *Please.*" Nicholas seemed desperate. "Why don't we *both* admit we have trouble expressing our emotions?"

"Because I don't!" Morgana stubbornly insisted.

"No. Not when you're expressing anger, you don't!"

"Do I have to say it to make you happy?" Morgana shook the phone at him. "All right. Is this clear enough? I love you!" she shouted.

"Juliette, darling, is that you?" a faint voice called from the receiver. Morgana stared at the phone and remembered the cake.

"No, this is Morgana Lawrence. About the cake—"

"Oh, Miss Lawrence," Mr. Carter chuckled. "You don't have to tell me you love me to get your cake. It's on its way. The truck got hung up in traffic. It'll be there anytime now."

"It'd better be," Morgana told him. "The reception has already started." She tried slamming down the receiver, but it was impossible with the antique-style instrument. She glared at Nicholas. "Well?"

"Your headband's crooked," he said softly, throwing her off kilter. "Let me straighten it for you." Placing warm hands on both sides of her face, he tenderly adjusted the beaded band. "I love you," he whispered, melting the last of Morgana's anger. She swayed toward him.

He'd finally said it, she thought. He'd told her the one thing she'd needed to hear for weeks. Throwing her arms around his neck, she whispered, "I love you, Nicholas."

Lips parted for his kiss, Morgana was rudely interrupted by a gruff voice.

"Where does this cake go?" A burly man in white coveralls stood at the door, balancing a huge box in his arms.

"Over there." Morgana dreamily motioned toward the empty spot on the table. The man moved away, and Morgana turned her attention to Nicholas. "Now," she said, only to be interrupted by an indignant protest.

"Hold on there! You can't do that!"

Morgana peered around Nicholas.

As the deliveryman positioned the cake, one of the caterers threatened him with a spatula. "Don't put it there. That's where we're going to put the finger sandwiches."

Regretfully moving out of her loved one's arms, Morgana straightened out the problem. "Leave the cake there, and put the sandwiches at the other end." Turning to Nicholas, she sighed. "I guess this isn't the time to talk."

"You mean I don't get to finish what I want to say to you *again?*"

Having forced her attention back to her work, Morgana only half heard his loud complaint. She was inspecting the growing crowd of people. Focusing on the refreshment table, she circled it, checking and rearranging things.

Following in her wake, Nicholas protested, "Morgana, I'm damn well going to finish my proposal this time!"

Morgana swallowed hard, remembering she'd called herself a fool for not considering his suggestion only half an

182

hour ago. "All right," she said, making up her mind. "I'll live with you if that's what you want."

Nicholas echoed, "All right? Live with me? That's not what I want. I mean, I do want us to live together." His voice rose with his exasperation. "What I want is to finish the proposal I started the night of Mari's wedding!"

A woman helping herself to some appetizers froze, one hand halfway to her mouth.

"Do we have to discuss contracts now?" Morgana hissed, not wanting to be the object of the woman's curiosity.

"I don't want to discuss contracts. I want to discuss us. I wanted to discuss us then, but somehow, I messed it up. I put things in the wrong order."

The woman's eyebrows were raised. She popped the hors d'oeuvre into her mouth and took a step closer. Morgana turned away and circled in the other direction, pushing right past Nicholas. She'd agreed to live with him, she thought angrily. What more did he want? And why did he insist on discussing it *now* when she obviously didn't want to?

"I don't like anyone trying to control me!" she told him through gritted teeth.

"I don't want to control you," Nicholas grumbled. "I want to *affect* you. Excuse me," he said, shouldering past a large man. "Will you stop, Morgana? I'm getting dizzy following you around in circles!"

Gazing at the tiny figures of the bride and groom at the top of the cake, Morgana stopped. She turned her attention to Nicholas and noted their growing audience. Behind him stood the man he'd edged by, the woman who was still eating, and a young couple.

"Now, about my proposal. I want you to know I tried again when I brought the contracts to your place and then a third time after our last . . . after our Spanish evening," he said, nervously glancing over his shoulder as a young woman stopped and stared.

"You asked me to live with you."

"No, I didn't ask you anything. You jumped to conclusions and never gave me the chance."

"And you told me my brain was warped," Morgana said accusingly, old hurts returning to make her edgy.

Nicholas sighed. "Maybe I ought to stick with black-and-white figures. It's the only means of expression I seem capable of handling properly." He pulled out a pen from his tweed jacket and wrote on one of the napkins. "Here. In businessman's black and white."

Morgana read the message aloud. "Will you marry me?" How could he do this to her? she wondered. Asking her in front of a growing crowd! And where was the candlelight and music? Glaring from the offensive missive to him, she asked tersely, "Am I supposed to write yes?"

Before Nicholas could answer, a middle-aged woman piped in, "That's an original way of proposing but not very romantic. You should get down on one knee."

Getting into the spirit, a large man grabbed a centerpiece from the nearest table and handed it to Nicholas. "A woman likes flowers when she's being courted," he whispered conspiratorially.

Flinging aside his ridiculous pink hat, Nicholas knelt and presented Morgana with the makeshift bouquet.

"Morgana, my love, I offer you these as I do my heart. Will you do me the honor of marrying me?"

Awestruck, Morgana froze. Nicholas was actually proposing in a wildly romantic manner, without concern for his own dignity. How could she resist when he looked so lovable in that silly costume, down on one knee, his hands raised in supplication?

184

"Yes!" Morgana shouted, suddenly shifting into action. She lunged at him while Nicholas was in the midst of rising, nearly knocking them to the floor. Steadying them both, Nicholas pulled her to him in an emotion-filled embrace.

His lips assaulted hers with a fervent passion, the likes of which she'd never before experienced. She threw her arms around his neck, but couldn't manage to get closer since the centerpiece sat between them, its wires pricking her stomach through the light material of her dress. Morgana did the best she could, forgetting the people around them for the moment.

Finally, the sound of approval—both cheering and applause—broke the spell. Startled, Morgana pulled away from Nicholas, but she didn't get far since the wires of the centerpiece linked them together. Blushing, Morgana loosened them from their clothing with shaky fingers. Looking up through the approving crowd, she moaned when she spotted the bride and groom at the door, surrounded by their dozen attendants. Their arrival had gone unnoticed!

"Good show!" Barney boomed from her side. He seemed highly satisfied with the situation. "I couldn't have staged it better myself."

"What entertainment," a young woman remarked. "Gee, Fantasy Weddings sure does a great job!"

"This wasn't a show." The middle-aged woman corrected her. "It's real romance." Then, turning to Nicholas and Morgana, she said, "I hope you'll be very happy."

"Thank you. Nicholas, the wedding party has arrived."

"Fear not," Barney interrupted. "My efficiency quotient has greatly improved. Trust me. I can carry on here. After your performance, anything I can arrange will be anticlimactic, but I can live with that," he said assuringly. "On to the love nest, you two."

"Thanks, Barney," Morgana said, kissing his cheek.

With the crowd now gathering around the newly married couple, no one seemed to notice when Morgana and Nicholas slipped out through the kitchen. Leaving the building, she tried to spot the silver sedan.

"Where's you car?"

"Right there."

He pointed. She stared.

Amid the half dozen or so antique cars they'd rented for the wedding party and immediate families—Fords, La Salles, Hudsons, and Cords—there stood one magnificent white Stutz Bearcat with massive whitewalls and unbelievable amounts of highly polished chrome to reflect the autumn sun. Its top was down.

"Our steed awaits," Nicholas told her, holding open the door.

After stepping onto the running board, Morgana lowered herself onto a white leather seat. "Oh, Nicholas, how romantic! Where did you find it?"

"A trade secret, my love." He got into the car and headed it for her apartment. "If I told, it would spoil the fantasy."

"I've always wondered what it was like to be a flapper." She sighed. "But, Nicholas, before we do any pretending, I've got to tell you the truth."

"If it's about business, I vote we forget it for now."

Love poured into her heart as she stared at his profile, his hair blowing in the wind. "I can't forget it. I've got some apologizing to do. I've thought some terrible things because of a bad experience."

"I know all about Miles," Nicholas told her.

"How do you . . . Barney."

"You can't be mad at Cupid." Nicholas chuckled. "Especially not when I *ordered* him to tell me everything he knew.

After that last fight I had to find out what was wrong. I wasn't going to lose you."

"Oh, Nicholas," she said, moving closer to him, finding comfort in the warmth of his body.

"You're lucky to have a friend like Barney. *We're* lucky," he amended. "If only I'd known the truth earlier! I can't say I've been totally innocent in this whole affair either."

"I wouldn't want you *innocent,*" Morgana told him, slipping her hand on his thigh. "Your experience is quite stimulating." The hand inched higher, and her lips found a sensitive spot on his neck.

"Hold on! I'm driving!"

"You could pull over to the side of the road."

"What I've got in mind can't be done on the side of a road . . . I don't think. Now behave yourself."

"Every party needs a pooper . . ." she sang, tucking her head on his shoulder.

"And you have the nerve to complain about *my* singing!"

In spite of his loud complaints, Morgana insisted on continuing all the way home. What a sight they made in the restored Stutz Bearcat, her ostrich feather blowing in the wind! They attracted a good deal of attention from other drivers as well as from pedestrians. Morgana waved to them, her heart singing, too. Nicholas was everything she could want in a man—and more.

By the time they entered the shop Nicholas was singing with her. But the moment the door closed behind them, he took her in his arms. "I love you, Morgana."

"And I love you."

"Don't ever stop telling me," he whispered, finding her lips with his own.

It was a tender embrace, one full of longing. Morgana felt her pulse flutter and wondered if Nicholas would always affect her this way. His lips were soft on hers, his tongue gentle and searching. It was a kiss that could last forever. Her body melded into his magic hands. Her knees grew weak as the fire sought her center and intensified. A liquid warmth flowed through her.

"I think we'd better go upstairs," she suggested weakly as his lips left a burning trail from her mouth to her ear. He was doing such delicious things to her! She pushed him away and grabbed his hand, pulling Nicholas past the office. "I vant to be alone . . . vith you!"

"Not yet." He stopped at the workroom doorway, refusing to let her drag him further.

"Vy not?" she asked huskily, trailing her free fingers down his chest, past his belt and lower.

"I haven't figured out my character yet."

"Well, I'm a sexy vamp, and you . . ."

Staring at his knee pants and pink socks, they broke into laughter.

"If I shut my eyes, I could pretend you're a gangster."

"Or a prohibitionist."

"No fun," she said complainingly. "Not romantic."

"Hm-m-m. Fun and romance." Nicholas thought for a minute, eyed her carefully, then snapped his fingers and demanded she wait right there. "And don't peek!"

Although Morgana remained where she was, she wondered how awful the penalty for peeking could be.

A minute later Nicholas lunged through the doorway dramatically, swathed in yards and yards of fabric. Ribbon wound around his forehead secured a headband.

Nicholas posed broadly, hands on hips. He rolled his eyes seductively, reminding Morgana of a silent movie character.

"The sheikh has come to claim his prize. To my tent, lovely wanton, where I will regale you with my passion. No, don't scream," he added, gesturing dramatically. "There's not another oasis for miles. No one will hear but the camels."

With a hand to her heart and a wrist to her forehead, Morgana the vamp swooned. Luckily her sheikh caught her in strong arms, picked her up, and strode through the workroom, heading for the stairs to her apartment.

"Be gentle with me," she cried faintly.

"I will. You needn't worry."

But Morgana wasn't worried. Whatever her future fantasies might be, she knew Nicholas would be there to help fulfill them.

EPILOGUE

Several months later, the following article appeared in the "Tempo" section of the Chicago *Tribune:*

UPDATE ON TRENDS: FANTASY FASHION

In an age when day-to-day reality is reflected in the austere clothing of the business world, a local firm sets new trends in magical romantic garb.

by Liz Colborne
Fashion Writer

For those who wish to express their creativity—and can afford it—Fantasy Weddings of Evanston designs dream weddings for romantic spirits.

Following their own philosophy, the owners of the firm, Morgana Lawrence and Nicholas Bedford, were wed last week in a ceremony illustrating the true nature of fantasy. Taking place in a local Gothic-style Unitarian church, the midnight candlelit ceremony was unexpectedly simple.

The bride appeared in a diaphanous pale blue gown, its translucence revealing an iridescent underdress. While slightly medieval in design, it had winglike wide sleeves and extended shoulders adding a futuristic touch. Was she Shakespeare's Titania? A benevolent Morgan le Fay? Or Princess Leia? The groom was a princely foil in a dark blue velvet tunic trimmed with silver and a pair of thigh-high boots. Both wore silver cords as headbands.

Their simple vows were taken in an atmosphere filled with hundreds of white candles and natural sprays of white flowers and were accompanied by the muted tones of a harp. In the choir loft the instrument was strummed by an aging red-headed cherub, his costume a set of real feathered wings.

The celebrants included former clients of Fantasy Weddings in addition to relatives and friends. All had been encouraged to come garbed as their favorite fantasy characters. And what a diverse display, proving that the definition of fantasy comes from within the individual.

All who attended feasted until dawn, when the bridal pair disappeared for their honeymoon—to never-never land?

Keep an eye on this new business. Incredibly creative, individually owned—a trend for the future? What we saw was a true fantasy wedding.

See companion article: an interview with Lawrence and Bedford.

LOOK FOR NEXT MONTH'S
CANDLELIGHT ECSTASY ROMANCES®:

282 TO REMEMBER LOVE, *Jo Calloway*
283 EVER A SONG, *Karen Whittenburg*
284 CASANOVA'S MASTER, *Anne Silverlock*
285 PASSIONATE ULTIMATUM, *Emma Bennett*
286 A PRIZE CATCH, *Anna Hudson*
287 LOVE NOT THE ENEMY, *Sara Jennings*
288 SUMMER FLING, *Natalie Stone*
289 AMBER PERSUASION, *Linda Vail*